CERBERUS THE TIGER

The Tiger Saga

Ezra Edmond

ISBN: 979-8-9929890-0-7 (Print)
       979-8-9929890-2-1 (eBook)
       979-8-9929890-1-4 (Hardcover)

DEDICATION

To my friends and family who have read or listened to various drafts about various tigers for nearly twenty years as the story of Cerberus finally emerged.

Without your support, *The Tiger Saga* wouldn't exist.

I dedicate this book to everyone who has been a part of this long journey.

Thank you.

ACKNOWLEDGMENTS

I am grateful for the authors, filmmakers, artists, teachers, and life experiences that have inspired me to become a storyteller. Stories fuel imagination and allow us to share new ideas, unique perspectives, and even inspire real-world change.

I hope that reading this story inspires you to tell your own.

CONTENTS

1

It had been about twenty-three days. Maybe a few more. Still, in these harsh conditions, he wasn't going to be able to survive much longer. Cerberus adjusted the leather straps that wrapped his paws. If today wasn't his birthday, it would be any day now. That is, if it hadn't already passed. There wasn't any real way to be sure.

It was cold, much colder than he was used to, and his breath chilled his whiskers as it exited his nostrils like white smoke. The sun would be down soon, and it was never a good idea to stay out after dark while being pursued by a relentless, blood-thirsty nocturnal monster. Wait… who was pursuing who again? Honestly, sometimes it felt like it went both ways.

Cerberus knew it was unreasonable to expect to find a safe place to stay every night, especially on a journey like this. The tips of his damp paws were close to freezing. Using a recently found rusted piece of sharp steel, he stripped damp bark off some nearby fallen branches, revealing dry wood beneath. Then, with the help of a stone and the same piece of steel, he sparked a cozy fire. He leaned up against a cliffside wall, so the only way anything unwelcome could approach would be from the front. If there was fire, there was safety.

Cerberus warmed his paws and placed several smooth stones around the base of the flames. Once they were heated, he would be able to wrap them in thick leaves and place them in his clothing to keep warm while he slept. He took some dry jerky from a satchel, wrapped a piece in a tea leaf, and began to chew. Even though it was incredibly dry, there was an interesting flavor that made the meal a bit more tolerable. Getting that degree in the culinary arts had really paid off.

Though the moment felt bleak, Cerberus couldn't help but think that his father, Leonidas, would be proud of him right now. Even with the odds stacked against him, Cerberus had managed to survive for about two months in this cold unfamiliar place. Though he never knew what tomorrow would bring, he knew Leonidas would have something to say in celebration of his imagination and ingenuity, and how embracing those traits are what had gotten him this far.

But now wasn't the time for self-congratulatory pats-on-the-back or the imagined satisfaction of long desired praise, though hopefully it soon would be. Through the shrouds of darkness, beyond the safety of fire, Cerberus could hear the disturbing, yet familiar, sounds of heavy breathing and crunching leaves in the trees around him. A pair of large eyes, flashed at him through the brush, their icy blue glow cutting through the darkness.

Soon, Cerberus thought. But not tonight.

With the fire as the only barrier limiting their confrontation, the eyes continued to stare at him from the darkness. A deep and threatening growl shook the ground, shaking the nearby branches and echoing Cerberus's thought.

Soon.

2

His life had changed a lot since the days when he was a kidden. Yet, as much as different as things were, he still fondly remembered growing up with his parents, Leonidas and Lucinda, and he would never forget the day Leonidas first took him to the new Animal Restoration Lab.

Leonidas had always loved two things: animals and fairy tales. When Cerberus was a kidden, Leonidas read to him every night before bed. They'd read old folktales, laughing about strange mythological animals like the *platypus*, but other times they would just read the latest think piece on the behavior of the creature known as *ice cream*, discussing what environment it could thrive best in. Once, Leonidas brought home a terrarium with rock salt, and Cerberus got to raise his own ice cream… at least until it got too big, and Lucinda made him release it back to the wild.

One afternoon, Leonidas came home with a bulletin board, and he and Cerberus spent the evening pinning up photos of their favorite animals. While it was easy for Cerberus to find pictures of all his favorites, Leonidas drew most of his. The results were hilarious. A *dolphin*, an *antelope*, and a *cow*? Nobody had ever heard of those animals before, at least not at Cerberus's school. Leonidas must have been making them all up. After all, he was creative, and that was one of the reasons that Lucinda usually cited when asked why she had married him.

Whenever Cerberus would laugh doubtingly at his dad's silly new animal ideas, Leonidas would double-down on their existence, telling

Cerberus that something wasn't necessarily fake just because he hadn't heard of it. But Cerberus took that with a grain of salt. Parents are supposed to encourage their kids to use their imaginations. If those silly animals were real, somebody else would've heard of them before. At the very least, Ricky would've. He was always learning about weird, random stuff.

Cerberus also loved when he was allowed to help Leonidas out in the lab, which was located just down the block from their home. Not in any monumental way, Cerberus was just a kidden, after all. He could hold the tools and keep his eye on the stove, but Leonidas always handled the big stuff. Whenever Leonidas was working, Cerberus would sit back and munch on jerky in awe. He wanted to be just like his dad when he grew up. What could be cooler than being an adult tiger, with his very own lab to do science in? Maybe he could even raise a young tiger of his own to hold the tools one day.

Occasionally, Leonidas would leave home for a long time, sometimes disappearing for weeks on end. Cerberus didn't know where he was going, but Lucinda assured him they were research trips critical to the success of the ARL, and that Leonidas always hurried back home to them as quickly as he could. Cerberus didn't understand why Leonidas couldn't do his research with the books they already had, and Lucinda would remind him that those books likely began with someone's research trips as well. Whenever Leonidas was away, Cerberus was trusted with access to the lab. Cerberus always looked forward to any opportunity to use the tools and materials in the lab to imagine and create to his heart's content, but he enjoyed it much more when his dad was able to be there imagining with him. After school, he would stay in the lab working on new projects until Lucinda called him for supper, using as many materials as he could get his paws on. His favorite days were when Leonidas returned because that meant he could share all the new ideas with him.

Though she always missed Leonidas when he was away, Lucinda admired how much these trips inspired Cerberus to want to become a scientist and go on research trips and adventures of his own someday. Occasionally, she would even let dinner get cold. She knew how much fun the little tiger was having in the lab, working on big ideas to share, and couldn't bear the idea of taking any of that fun away from him.

Encouraged by his parents, Ricky, the panther kidden down the block, often joined Cerberus in the lab, where he quickly found himself feeling quite at home. His natural inclination towards science and learning paired well with Cerberus's powerful imagination and the two formed a strong bond quickly. There was no better afternoon for the two kiddens than when Leonidas would gather them for *Story Time*, a fun celebration of learning where he would describe the latest animals of eras past that he had been researching. Cerberus and Ricky would draw their favorite strange animals based off Leonidas's descriptions, imagining what the animals may have looked like and what they may have been up to back in their day.

Together, Cerberus and Ricky would laugh about *the giraffe* and *the bear*, wondering why anyone would think these animals had ever existed to begin with. Why did a giraffe have horns? Leonidas said they weren't horns, they were something called *ossicones*, but either way they seemed hilariously impractical! At least a bear sounded like it was strong and could probably lift lumber, stop a runaway vehicle, or help someone move their fridge. But there was no way a giraffe could ever wear a suit and fit in at the office—not with a neck as long as Leonidas had described. Whenever Leonidas returned from his research trips, he loved how the kiddens would gather around him, excited to hear the stories behind his latest discovery.

After one particularly long research trip, Leonidas called for Cerberus to join him in the lab. As he arrived and sat down to hear the news, he noticed the glint in Leonidas's eye and knew something was different right away.

"Cerberus, I've done it."

Leonidas couldn't hold back his smile as he held up a small, sealed vial. Cerberus's eyes grew wide with excitement, even though he couldn't see exactly what was inside.

"Inside this vial is undeniable proof that the strange animals of eras past were real, just like you and I always thought."

"You and I, and Ricky," said Cerberus.

"Yes, and Ricky."

Leonidas put a paw on Cerberus's shoulder.

"But I want to do this next step with you, my son. With the research I've acquired, your strong imagination, and the proof in this very vial, we can finally finish building the ARL."

"And then we'll be able to bring an animal back?"

"Little one, we'll be able to do far more than bring an animal back. Together we'll be able to accomplish all our wildest dreams. But I thought we could start with a giraffe."

A giraffe! Cerberus couldn't wait. Ever since Leonidas had started the ARL, all Cerberus had wanted to do was work there with him. Changing the world every day with fabulous inventions and marvelous animals. He could barely fall asleep that night; the big day was finally closer than ever.

3

Cerberus stoked the embers of the fire as the morning sun peeked through the trees, buttery light spilling over him. Another safe night. What was this now, day twenty-two? Or maybe twenty-three?

It didn't matter. Time was irrelevant anyway.

Cautiously, Cerberus got to his feet. The beast was gone, confined to the shadows, and it was time to get moving.

Climbing a sturdy tree, Cerberus could see over the forest canopy which helped him get his bearings. In the distance, he could make out the silhouette of a rustic city, where smoke appeared to rise from assorted chimneys greeting the day. Cerberus marked it down on a piece of parchment and climbed back down to the Earth. He checked the nearby trail he'd been following, a ragged path of smashed trees and foliage that continued endlessly through the wood, heading right in that very same city's direction. Maybe there he'd be able to figure out his next steps. Maybe he would even find somewhere to eat. A hot plate of real food would be a welcome addition to his day. Maybe they even gave you something special on your birthday. Not that it *was* his birthday. But it might be. Who knew?

The woods were quieter than Cerberus would have expected. The occasional bird whistled, and branches creaked in the wind, but otherwise he was mostly surrounded by silence. He wondered if the woods had always been like this, or if it was his doing. Or maybe the beast in the shadows at night wasn't only there at night. Maybe nighttime was the only time it could be seen.

Stopping by a stream, Cerberus dipped his paws and washed his face. He then took a sip. He knew he shouldn't. Leonidas had warned him about the natural water quality when he was a kidden. *"Only drink the water in the city,"* was his mantra. That water was pure. The water outside, not so much. But when you don't have a choice, what else are you supposed to do? If he ever made it back home, he knew there were cures available for water-borne illnesses. That would just have to be a problem for later.

Following the river to a fork, Cerberus continued to the left. That was where the city should be. He marked his parchment for future reference. At a clearing, the path became worn and familiar. Voices could be heard faintly in the distance, growing louder as he approached. Finally, he crossed over a hilltop, and below, the whole city sprawl was revealed. Though it had been cold for most of his journey, the weather had been clear. Here, Cerberus noticed that the entire town was covered in a blanket of freshly fallen snow.

A group of kiddens of various ages and species played together in the town square, throwing snowballs, as the adults went about their daily routine—but everyone stopped in their tracks as they watched Cerberus approach. Sure, Cerberus was quite a handsome tiger, if he did say so himself, but these weren't those kinds of looks. These folks hadn't seen anyone quite like him before. His dress was unfamiliar, and his cold stare and smell reeked of someone who hadn't spoken to anyone else in at least twenty-three days.

Cerberus lifted a paw in a light wave, forcing his first smile in weeks. A small tiger kidden stared back, frozen in his tracks. There was no smile back. Uncomfortable, but knowing he had to push on regardless, Cerberus continued walking leaving the confused citizens behind.

A large stone pub sat in the center of a worn town square, neatly nestled behind a statue of a regal, hulking figure sitting on a massive throne. Cerberus figured that must be the king of this region, or at least a king from generations past. Feeling like he was being watched, Cerberus scanned the snowy landscape, settling on the mountain range at the city's edge. There, resting on a ledge, a massive, dark castle loomed. Though it appeared ancient and unoccupied, Cerberus could swear he saw a flicker of fire briefly in a window.

Then again, it could just be light refracting off the snow.

Craving warmth, Cerberus made his way towards the pub. Nearby, a squad of soldiers watched him cautiously. But there was no need to overreact. He could tell he was getting closer than ever, and nothing was going to stop him now.

4

O n Cerberus's eighth birthday, at precisely 6:43am, Leonidas woke him up and announced that it was finally time. After a late night of work, the ARL was officially functional, and it was time to bring back the first missing animal. Cerberus had never jumped out of bed faster.

By 7:49am, they were at the lab. Leonidas made sure that nobody else was there that could disturb their special moment. It was time to bring back Cerberus's favorite missing animal, the first one that the Animal Restoration Lab would recover: the giraffe. This was bound to be a historic moment, and Leonidas and Cerberus were going to do it together.

Of course, Cerberus had told Ricky about the undeniable proof that Leonidas had recently brought home. And though giddy, impatient, and beyond excited, Ricky was understanding when he was told that the big day was intended to be a father-son moment. Cerberus assured him that as soon as they had a successful result, he could come over immediately to see for himself, and like a good friend should be, Ricky was accepting of that game plan.

As Cerberus performed a final inspection of Leonidas's latest work on the equipment, Leonidas donned a heavy protective hazard suit, and brought over a thick, black case, made of a dark, shell-like material.

"The other critical piece to our experiment," Leonidas said as he set it down next to the sealed vial he had shared with Cerberus a few nights earlier.

Though Cerberus still didn't quite understand what these two elements were, once placed next to each other he could hear a surreal humming emanating between the vial and the case, causing both the vibrate in response to each other. Even without any additional knowledge, it was clear to even a casual viewer that these items contained some powerful stuff.

Leonidas called the stuff in the case *MonFus*—short for *Monumental Fusion*. It wasn't just an energy source; it acted as a stabilizer, binding lost genetic material to a viable form. At least, that was the theory. Even he wasn't entirely sure how it worked yet and said that it could only be truly understood with much more additional time and study. Still, what they knew about the stuff currently was enough for what they hoped to achieve today.

From the safety of his hazard suit, Leonidas cracked the shell case open, and transferred the bright blue MonFus extract into the ARL's application deck. Once complete, Cerberus ran the cables, connecting the deck to the frame of their portal. According to Leonidas, this should all be a simple yet exciting process. Once they loaded the giraffe proof into the machine, the portal would open. The device would send out a signal to locate a giraffe, and once it did, they would isolate the instance and pull it through the portal and into the lab.

"If this first test is successful, we can try to replicate it and find a second giraffe of opposite gender," Leonidas muttered, as he typed a long numerical code onto a handheld signal calibration device. "Then nature will be able to take its course from there."

Once the signal was calibrated, Leonidas finally cracked the sealed vial open, and Cerberus could see what this undeniable proof was. It was curious; indeed, a single golden drop of amorphous liquid, pulsing with a calm and gentle rhythm.

Leonidas transferred the proof into the reader, which was adjacent to the application deck, connected to the portal through its own designated wiring.

"Alright, little one, safety first."

Leonidas helped Cerberus into the viewing room, an airlocked chamber adjacent to the lab. It had a large double-enforced window, which would allow Cerberus to watch the experiment from a safe, protected environment. He was just a kidden, after all, and Leonidas wasn't about to risk exposing him to such intensive and untested science at such a young age. Cerberus understood that safety always came first, and even though he couldn't be in the room with Leonidas, he wasn't upset about it at all. He was finally about to meet his first giraffe! Maybe one day he and the giraffe would be able to pick apples, see over tall buildings, and wash windows together, like long-necked creatures and their friends did in the books he had at home.

Preparations had taken all day, and now, just as the cover of night fell, Leonidas finished entering one last string of code into the system and it was officially time to begin. With a deep breath, Leonidas pulled down a big activation lever, and the machine spun to life.

Cerberus watched through the double-enforced window with giddy anticipation as the golden giraffe proof was pulled into the system from one side as the MonFus was pulled into the other, meeting at a center window above the portal door. The ball of golden liquid pulsed and glowed red, dissolving quickly into the MonFus. The blue MonFus pulsed, prickled, and swelled, as the red disappeared, and after a few more swirls, the combined elements turned a bright, rich purple.

Leonidas adjusted his goggles and pulled out his handheld *UltraNine* laser. Cerberus loved when Leonidas would use the UltraNine. It was no larger than a large whiteboard marker and had a diode at the end capable of creating a focused beam of light. Using the UltraNine meant that some very delicate, precise work lay ahead.

"The Creator's Pen in action," Leonidas said turning towards Cerberus. Cerberus couldn't hear him through the glass, but he knew what his father was saying, since this was far from the first time he had said it. With a smile, Leonidas powered up the beam and adjusted the small dials, narrowing the focus to a molecular level. He pointed it at the MonFus and with quick, clean work, cut and shaped the molecules with a satisfied grin across his face. Cerberus remembered just how proud Leonidas was on the day that he had finished inventing it. Calling it *The Creator's Pen* was just a joke between the two of them. Leonidas called all pens *The Creator's Pen* because all pens could be used to express imagination and creativity, even if they weren't groundbreaking tools designed for meaningful advancements in micro-science. To Leonidas, it was always about the paw that held the tool that made something special, not the tool itself. Leonidas made quick work with it, confirming that the bonds between the giraffe proof and MonFus were fully formed. Now the purple MonFus combination glowed as cracks of blue energy bolts flickered around it.

With a cool, casual, wink at the little tiger, Leonidas spun the UltraNine around in his paw, shut it off, and pocketed it once again. He then pulled a second lever, and the portal generation process began.

The energized purple concoction seeped down into a series of tubes. Leonidas fine-tuned the controls, and the portal began to glow. His paw hesitated over a gauge flickering erratically—just for a moment. A miscalibration? No, the energy levels were steady. He shook off the unease and focused. This was history in the making. Not wanting to miss a second, Cerberus watched the portal intensely.

Slowly, it began to swirl open.

Purple light spilled out of the portal and across Leonidas. Soon, the gates to either side clanked into their locking mechanisms, and inside the portal, something began to materialize.

Cerberus watched in anticipation as fuzzy shapes formed in the purple fog, shifting into new forms almost as quickly as they revealed themselves. Cerberus thought some of the shapes looked familiar. Was that one a *rhino*? Who knew—it was already turning into something else! Finally, with a ding, the colors shifted and settled as a final silhouetted shape became clear.

A head.

A long neck.

Leopard-spotted velvety yellow-and-brown splotched skin.

Cerberus couldn't believe it. A giraffe!

Leonidas carefully approached the portal. He knew the giraffe would be out of its element, and it was crucial to keep it calm on entry. Cerberus wanted to run out and throw a beautiful long scarf around its neck, but he knew he had to wait until Leonidas gave him the all-clear. That, and he needed someone to open the airlock, as there wasn't a handle on the inside.

Leonidas pulled out a snack for their new friend, a few berries saved from yesterday's breakfast. He held his paw out towards the giraffe shadow, and slowly the newly formed animal poked its curious head out through the portal.

It was beautiful. Cerberus watched through the glass in amazement as the giraffe stretched its neck into the room and lowered its head into Leonidas's paw to eat. Cerberus marveled at its purple tongue, tremendously long eyelashes, and brown-and-yellow patches. He had never seen anything like it before.

"I'm going to name you Lupita," Cerberus thought.

"Come on, my friend."

Leonidas was having a hard time convincing the giraffe to fully exit the machine. It seemed willing to risk its neck, but nothing else—not even a hoof—had yet to pass through the portal.

Maybe it wasn't finished forming yet. There wasn't much MonFus left in the machine. Maybe they needed more. But suddenly the erratic gauge flickered again and —CLANG—the lock released. The portal gates began to close. Startled, the giraffe looked around the room in a panic, swinging her neck back and forth. Leonidas struggled between trying calm her with one paw while pushing to hold the portal gates open with his other.

Cerberus called through the glass, wanting to help. But being trapped in a soundproof, airlocked room isn't good for that. Besides, Leonidas was far too busy with the chaos to stop to let him out. Grabbing a steel rod, Leonidas jammed the portal gates open—and seconds later had both his paws around the giraffe, comforting and calming her. Maybe she'd go back to eating her berries in peace.

However, the rod wasn't enough to hold the gates. Recognizing the obstruction, an alarm sounded, and the security measures clicked in, adding additional pressure to the pistons.

The rod snapped, rocketing across the room and into the

MonFus container, shattering it instantly. Purple sprayed across the lab, dusting the walls, Leonidas, and the terrified giraffe. Cerberus watched in horror as the giraffe reared its head violently in reaction, throwing Leonidas across the room and into the thick glass window that separated him and Cerberus, leaving a huge crack in the glass. Leonidas sank down out of view. With a final slam, the gates shut as much as they could, given that they had a giraffe's neck in the way. Though smoke still emanated from the gap between them, the room went silent.

In the viewing room, Cerberus didn't know what to do. The door was still locked from the outside, and though the viewing window had cracked, the crack wasn't weak enough for the kidden to break the rest of the window himself. He looked through the fractured glass at the remains of the lab and at the giraffe, who was stuck between the portal and their world. There was no sign of Leonidas, and who knew how long it would take someone to find them here?

With all hope lost, Cerberus tucked himself into the corner of the room as tears began to roll down his cheeks.

But all was not lost, and suddenly a paw grabbed the windowsill. Leonidas pulled himself up. He was bruised and covered in MonFus, but otherwise he seemed all right.

"Don't worry little one, I'm okay."

Leonidas looked over at the motionless giraffe, and then back through the window to his son. "All right, let's get you out of there."

Leonidas made his way to the airlock keypad and began the unlocking procedure. Cerberus ran to the door. He couldn't wait to hug his dad and get out of this lab forever. Maybe he and Lupita weren't meant to be friends after all, and he was sorry for everything that had just happened to her.

The airlock clicked and unsealed. Cerberus pushed the door open—

And saw something move out of the corner of his eye.

Lupita.

But it wasn't normal movement... and the MonFus had disappeared. Had it been absorbed into her skin?

But either way, Lupita was moving. Violently.

"Uh, dad," Cerberus whispered. "What's happening?"

The portal gates began to shake, and Cerberus froze in his tracks. Lupita's eyes shot open with a start, and she started to purr. Or was it a cough? No, it was definitely a *roar*.

Leonidas turned around in time to see Lupita's smooth, flat teeth extend into sharp fangs. Her jaw stretched, and her neck grew, pushing the portal open. Soon, her neck would be too wide to fit.

"Stay here," Leonidas ordered. "I need to shut off the machine!"

He pulled the airlock door shut, trapping Cerberus again.

Cerberus watched as Lupita's ossicones transformed into gnarled horns. The giraffe turned long-necked monster lunged, slamming into the airlock door as Leonidas leapt out of the way. He quickly scrambled towards the back of the portal, struggling to reach the machine's main power switch. The frame of the portal began to crack as Lupita's swollen, scaly neck pushed against the barrier. Blue electricity surged around the machine, flashing bright neon beams as it collided with the splashing MonFus.

The giraffe formerly known as Lupita was no more. That was certain. Transformation complete, a terrifying lizard's tongue whipped from its mouth, wrapping around Leonidas's leg. It retracted, pulling the older tiger toward its shiny new fangs.

Cerberus wished an adult would cover his eyes, but since he was trapped behind the airlock door with the only available adult wrapped in a lizard's tongue on the other side, this wasn't possible. So, too transfixed to do anything else, he just watched in horror. The beast slid further through the unstable portal gates, cracking the mechanical structure, and causing further malfunction. It seemed like its neck went on for eternity. Passing the airlock, the beast's piercing blue eyes looked straight through the cracked glass and into Cerberus's soul. Cerberus felt a chill, and a horrible feeling that he had never known before slithered down his spine.

The beast whipped its head around with a frightening scream. Turning, Cerberus could see that Leonidas had managed to pull his UltraNine from his pocket and had stabbed the creature's other eye, causing the glowing blue to sizzle into black.

"Hang on, little one, I'll get us out of this!" Leonidas called.

The beast whipped its head back and forth, smashing everything in the room even further beyond repair. It reared up, slamming Leonidas through one of the two skylights in the ceiling. Cerberus watched as his father flew, UltraNine still in paw. Strangely, the beast didn't watch Leonidas at all, instead it kept its eyes locked on Cerberus in the airlock as it continued to pull its body through the warped and busted portal.

Midair, above the lab, Leonidas thought quickly. He looked down. The beast wasn't watching. If he positioned the UltraNine laser perfectly, the fall should give him enough force to ram the tool through the beast's head, stopping it once and for all. Leonidas oriented himself as best he could as he descended. Through the second skylight—wait, what was *that*? A flash of blue? No, the beast was still watching Cerberus.

Cerberus watched as, the beast's dull eye flickered back to a bright blue, and it seemed to smile. Then suddenly, with a crash, a second head shot through the portal door and up through the second skylight, shattering it. A second tongue wrapped around Leonidas. Instantly, it swallowed him whole.

As shattered glass rained down into the room, the beast's second head roared into the night sky. It dove swiftly, smashing against the airlock door. Cerberus retreated to the back of the viewing room in fear. It was only a matter of time until one of the two heads smashed through.

Sparks of lightning gave way to fire as the beast did everything it could to get at Cerberus, but as the heat and flames grew, the creature's energy seemed to drain. Moving slowly, it seemed to be giving up, favoring moving its body away from the heat over capturing its target. One head began to move towards the portal, dragging the other behind it. The first head had an almost fearful look in its eyes. The scales along its body started to singe and smoke. The second head looked back into Cerberus's eyes as it was dragged back, seemingly blaming him for this. It pulled its other head, trying to thrash against the airlock window once again.

"HEY!" a small voice called.

The monster's eyes flashed across the room towards the

entrance. Quickly, it whipped around and slithered its massive body through the portal as Ricky ran into the lab. Before he could get a clear look at the two-headed snake beast, the second head was dragged through the portal gate, and with a final tongue-lash, it was gone. Now unobstructed, the portal closed for good.

Ricky pulled an emergency lever, and the fire sprinklers came on, subduing the roaring fire to nothing more than smoldering ashes in a matter of moments. Ricky ran through the remains of the lab, avoiding the loose cables and surging electricity. He opened the airlock door, but Cerberus pulled him in quickly, almost shutting it again.

"No! It could come back!"

Ricky put his foot in the doorway. No way were they both getting stuck in here after all that.

"What was that thing, anyway?"

"I don't know! What are you doing here?"

"I wanted to meet the giraffe too. Where's your dad?"

Cerberus's lack of words said it all, and Ricky fell silent.

5

The next four years weren't easy for the Tiger family. After coming to terms with the fact that Leonidas wouldn't be returning home any time soon, if ever, Lucinda had hidden away the bulletin board of fantastical animals and forbade any more talk of *"that nonsense."* Lucinda never asked Cerberus for details. She didn't need to. Whatever had happened in that lab had taken her husband—Cerberus's father—away, and that was enough. In her opinion, discussing the accident wouldn't change anything so there was no point to it.

During this time, she remarried, this time to an older boar who didn't believe in any of that nonsense either. A few years before, she couldn't have imagined being with anyone of the sort; but now, the pair felt made for each other.

At Cerberus's pleading, his mother agreed to leave the lab untouched—but only after he promised to invest his time and money into a *"more practical"* field instead: culinary training. Everyone needed food, and it wasn't dangerous. Though he looked forward to learning the science of making tasty and beautiful meals, Cerberus, still just a young kidden of twelve, never imagined his father's work would have led him to this moment. The best culinary program was in an entirely different city, meaning Cerberus would need to move away from the place he had called home his entire life. He promised his mother he would make the most of the opportunity even though it wasn't a promise he would've made under different circumstances.

Luckily for Cerberus, Ricky hadn't been forced to make the same promise and saw an opportunity. So as Lucinda packed up the house to make room for her new married life with Henry B. Orenthall, and as Cerberus packed up his ice cream terrarium and set off for a ten yearlong immersive program at the culinary academy across the country, Ricky took over the lab, inspired to complete Leonidas's work. He wrote periodically to Cerberus over those next ten years, giving him updates about the restoration of the lab. But Cerberus would rarely write back, due to the heavy workload at the Culinary Academy—as well as not wanting to upset his mother.

Cerberus stayed at the top of his class the entire program. Cooking felt like second nature—the way combining ingredients mirrored his father's old experiments was almost comforting, yet different enough to not stir up the terrible memories.

He also made a new friend in Dot, a piglet who frequently worked late in the Culinary Labs as well. Cerberus would often ask her to join him on his walk home any time it was dark after classes were over, because whenever he walked home at night by himself, he would feel an unpleasant tingle in his spine—and sometimes could swear that those glowing blue eyes from long ago were still watching him from the shadows.

No matter how many years went by, the feeling never felt any weaker than it had been since the first time he felt it. On those nights, he was eternally grateful for Dot's company. Dot liked walking at night with Cerberus too, because he never scoffed at her more outlandish ideas for culinary combinations. He believed everything was possible, especially when others didn't, and she was grateful for his endless support and encouragement.

***

Finally, graduation day arrived, and the students couldn't believe how quickly the ten years had gone by.

Lucinda and Henry had taken a cross-country carriage to witness Cerberus's graduation, and they had brought along Stephenson, the newest addition to the family. At six years old, Stephenson was already showing interest in the culinary trade, and Henry thought seeing someone graduate the Academy would be good for him.

Cerberus and Dot graduated at the top of their class to roaring applause, and samples of their thesis projects were handed out for the audience to sample. Lucinda thought both courses were amazing, but Henry didn't like Dot's outrageous flavor combinations. They were a bit too outlandish and non-traditional for his tongue to understand; but then again, Henry had always been a bit of a bore anyway, so it wasn't a surprise.

After graduation, Cerberus said a difficult goodbye to Dot and joined his family for the carriage ride back home. Passing beautifully overgrown ruins along the way, the trip home was something to behold. Ten years before, on his ride to the program, all he had wanted to do was get away from his home, but now, as he made his way back to the place he had once loved so much, he was finally able to take in the surrounding landscape as he looked out at the sights in an effort to distract himself from Henrys constant praise and recounting of Stephenson's many accomplishments.

Passing by so many overgrown ruins when traveling from a place as developed as the Culinary Academy and heading towards the city he had been born, was very interesting. Though there wasn't much documentation on the history of these areas, Cerberus's mind wandered, and he imagined the glory of what these sites once were. Who lived here? What did they do in their day to day lives? There was no way to know, but it was fun to imagine a time before his own.

The ride was a long one. With Stephenson's betterment in mind, Lucinda had arranged for a few different nights stays along the journey. Each one was at a different historic, beautiful location, but every night, regardless of the quality of hotel, campsite, or bed & breakfast, Cerberus still felt the same unsettling tingle. He missed having Dot at his side to help reassure him, Henry didn't care to understand, Stephenson was far too young, and he didn't want to worry his mother or even bring it up to her at all. Some nights it was stronger than others, but there was never a night when the feeling wasn't there. And, as much as his family couldn't relate to his feeling, he was happy that they were there. He didn't know if he'd ever be able to spend a night by himself again.

"That's okay," Cerberus concluded. "Nobody wants to be alone at night anyway."

6

As the carriage pulled into Lucinda and Henry's new driveway back home, the only thing on Cerberus's mind was finding Ricky. Ricky had regretfully declined the invitation to the culinary graduation due to a breakthrough he was about to accomplish at the ARL, and Cerberus couldn't wait to sneak away from Lucinda and over to his father's old lab so he could finally see what Ricky had been up to.

Though Ricky was the same age as Cerberus, he had thrown himself headfirst into his research work at the ARL, having been deemed a prodigy. Now known as the youngest scientist ever to work in such complex fields, Cerberus couldn't escape news about his old friend and his accomplishments. In another lifetime, Ricky's path may have been Cerberus's own. While he was genuinely excited to see the work that Ricky had been accomplishing, it was very hard to reconcile those feelings.

Ten years. He could have come back sooner. Should have. But stepping through that door meant facing everything he'd buried.

The tiger knew it would be strange, and likely very painful, to return to the place where everything in his life had changed so suddenly. But he couldn't run away from his past forever. So, after telling Lucinda and Henry he was going to take Stephenson to see a play in celebration of his return home, he dropped Stephenson off at a friend's house and snuck off to his real destination, the site of the horrible accident that had shifted his future forever.

✳✳✳

"Welcome home, Big C!"

Ricky was waiting in front of the lab, ten years older but with the same goofy smile that Cerberus knew as a kidden slapped across his panther face. There was barely any time to catch up before Ricky jumped straight to the point.

"I've changed up the place a lot, since… you know…" Ricky averted his gaze, just for a second. "But are you sure you're ready to come back in here? I mean, not like you need permission from me or anything. It's still basically your lab, of course. Even if I'm working here."

As Ricky rambled nervously, Cerberus looked around the doorway. Though the old paint was worn, and hinges showed slight signs of rust, it still looked almost the same as it did the last time he had visited with Leonidas. From the outside of the lab, nobody would ever guess how much damage, destruction, and sadness the inside of the lab had experienced that night. Cerberus wondered if anyone who looked at him in the years since that fateful night would ever assume the same.

Cerberus took a deep breath. "Don't worry, I'm ready."

Ricky held the door open as Cerberus stepped inside. Walking cautiously through the once familiar threshold, he couldn't believe his eyes. All the damage had been not only restored, but all the machinery had been given full upgrades. Various experiments were underway throughout the facility, each clearly in different stages of development, with a flurry of lively lab assistants working diligently across them.

One of the latest breakthroughs Ricky was excited to show off was the *Duckling*. Cerberus marveled at its yellow plumage, orange bill, and deep black eyes, nearly getting lost in their gaze.

"My dad used to tell me folk tales about the Duckling! How did you manage to bring one back?" Cerberus asked curiously.

"Oh, I haven't tried to bring anything back," Ricky quickly said. "I made this one from scratch. It'll be a duckling forever—and the funniest thing is, they make perfect carriage drivers. For whatever

23

reason, we discovered they possess an instinct to chauffeur. In the future, I see a world of driverless, duckling-driven carriages for everyone. Never worry about falling asleep at the reins again."

"Wait, you haven't tried to bring anything back?" Cerberus was confused. "Why?"

"There's not enough MonFus. There is a little left over from…" Ricky pivoted quicky. "But I don't have any idea where your dad found the original source."

Ricky held out a paw and the duckling climbed up to his shoulder to perch.

"I've been searching for more MonFus for years, but I figure that, until I can find the source, I shouldn't waste it. So, in the meantime, I have reallocated the ARL resources towards building new animals from scratch. They may not be exactly like what they once were, but can you imagine what the world will be like with these animals being a part of it once again?"

Cerberus admired the little duckling, who hopped off Ricky's shoulder with an expression that could only be described as *"rearing to get behind the wheel."* As much as Cerberus had felt unsure about ever returning to this place, he couldn't help but look at Ricky's accomplishment in awe. Leonidas had always dreamed of a world that these animals were a part of, and now Ricky was making those dreams come true.

"Incredible," Cerberus breathed.

"Well, it's not like I can take credit for all of this," Ricky said modestly. "Besides the help of these talented lab assistants, I never could've done this without your dad's work and journals. Which led me to the big breakthrough."

Ricky led Cerberus across the lab and into the room where it all had happened ten years ago. Cerberus felt a slow tingle across his spine, and hesitated.

"Don't worry," Ricky assured him. "It's safe here."

Ricky explained that over the years he had investigated and confirmed that the animals they used to study and fantasize about were all actually real animals, but he didn't know from when, or where they had gone. Even in the information he had found, there was very little documentation on the details. All Ricky could figure out was that once upon a time there were certain animals existing, and then, suddenly, there weren't anymore—as if they had evaporated away in an instant.

"But they're all still here," Ricky said excitedly. He pulled up a chart, graphing energy signals, showing different peaks and lows. "Using residual data from the old portal, I've been able to chart the energy of all the animals we used to imagine bringing back when we were kiddens. The *platypus*, the *bear*, the *cow*, all of them. Sometimes the energy pulses stronger than at other times, but it's never completely gone. And when the pulses are really high, there's a physical reaction wherever it's located. I think that's how your dad was able to find the giraffe proof."

"So, you're saying all the animals we thought to be imaginary are actually real, and their energy is just… floating all around us?" Cerberus was skeptical, even though this was somehow the most logical explanation he had ever heard.

"Yeah—it really seems that one day, they just evaporated. Or at least their bodies did."

He hustled to a cabinet and pulled out a wrapped folder.

"And look at this."

Ricky opened the folder and pulled out a series of scans from books and historical documentation. Cerberus had been away from this sort of thing for a long while, and the sheets didn't all make sense immediately. However, there was one creature drawn, charted, and noted on all of them, something that Cerberus could never forget, even ten years later. The two-headed beast, formerly known as Lupita the giraffe, that had come through the portal and eaten his father.

"I've been doing research, and throughout history, whenever this sort of energy surge has been charted, this beast has been spotted. It's even in some of the earliest known histories, dating back what must be hundreds of years, if not thousands. I don't know what it is, but it's always there."

"Maybe its job is to stop us from bringing creatures back to times where they don't belong," Cerberus wondered aloud. "Maybe that's why it ate my dad."

"Maybe it didn't eat him."

"Of course it ate him. I was there; I saw it. Even you were there."

"Maybe it just took him. To another time."

Cerberus's thoughts only went to one place. "So, what you're saying is that we might be able to get him back?'

The plan was simple in its complexity. Ricky had charted out the fact that long-lost *bunny* energy had been located surging across town in a senior citizen home, and based on previous charts, it was due to peak in a three nights time. If Ricky and Cerberus could extract the energy at its peak, they'd be able to capture a proof and refine it back at the lab, using their technology to adapt it into a substance that, in theory, could work very similarly to MonFus. Once modified, using the newly reconstructed portal generator in the lab, they could open the portal again, and hopefully use it to bring back Leonidas. They would have to be careful not to overload the system; with too powerful of a surge, and according to the history they had both witnessed ten years prior, the two-headed beast with the glowing blue eyes would return once again.

7

Three nights later, at 11:57pm, Cerberus waited to meet Ricky in front of the Heartland Senior Citizen's Home, where seventy-eight-year-old Alberto Broccolini had been reported to be exhibiting increasingly strange behavior. Of course, Cerberus and Ricky knew that this must be related to the strange surge in bunny energy, but the nurses were never going to comprehend that explanation for his psychological duress.

At 12:01am, Ricky arrived in a town car, driven by one of his new ducklings. After an unsuccessful attempt to parallel park that lasted seven minutes and thirteen seconds, Ricky got out of the vehicle, instructing the duckling to *"keep it running"* until they returned. While driving came naturally to the ducklings, parking had turned out to be a much harder thing to teach. Maybe someday.

Popping the trunk, Ricky pulled out two lab coats, a canister for the soon-to-be-gathered bunny proof, and a strange device called a *Proof Extractor* that looked like a megaphone crossed with a spinning wheel. Cerberus had seen similar devices in the ARL back when he was a kidden, but this was clearly an upgraded version.

"We have to calibrate this extractor just right," Ricky cautioned. "Too strong, and we could rip away more than just the proof."

Lab coats on, they entered the home. After convincing the nurses that they were specialized doctors from a nearby city hired by Alberto's family to provide a second opinion, they were shown down a long, dimly lit hallway to his room. Passing the rooms of other residents, Cerberus peeked through their open doors in observation. He saw an old tortoise brushing an equally old moose's grey hair, a lion playing chess from both sides of the table, and an elderly blue heron surrounded by relatives who were introducing him to the youngest member of the family.

A bell rang, startling Cerberus. As a rumbling sounded above him, Cerberus watched as fresh vegetables, orange juice, and a bowl of brown pudding slid through a series of chutes and into everyone's individual rooms. As the residents happily ate their 12:15am snack, Cerberus thought that, contrary to popular belief, this didn't seem like a bad place to live. A poster advertised morning massages, and apparently, you could use the bedside handset to "dial three" at any time for a fresh cup of hot cocoa delivered to you by a motivational speaker. However, a motivational speech was not included unless you paid an additional fee.

Reaching the end of the hall, they entered Alberto's room. Though pudding and hot cocoa surrounded his bedside, the elderly Alberto stared straight ahead ignoring their pleasant scents. His eyes were vacant and unblinking.

"He's been like this for a few days," the nurse said. "He was doing fine until his most recent weekly examination. When we put him in the scanner, he started muttering something about magnets and then snapped into this state. I'm so glad you're here; his family misses him, and all this pudding is going to go bad if he doesn't eat it soon. However..."

The nurse pushed the bedside vegetable delivery button, and a fresh batch slid out of the nearby chute. Alberto's nose wiggled, and his mouth dropped opened ever so slightly.

"... he's still eating his vegetables, so at least he's healthy in that regard."

The nurse lifted a carrot up to Alberto's mouth. With a quick nose twitch, Alberto leaned forward and consumed the carrot. But, as soon as it was gone, he instantly returned to his previous state.

Ricky and Cerberus looked at each other knowingly. Even if they didn't know why, Alberto clearly was connected to the source of the bunny energy surge. Ricky assured the nurse there was nothing to worry about, and asked for them to move Alberto into the examination room and strap him down safely so that they could conduct their exam. The nurse wheeled Alberto in, asked if anything further was needed, and when Ricky replied "No," the nurse departed, assumedly to go and tend to someone else in the facility.

As soon as she was gone, Ricky leaped into action, eyes darting around the room.

"Okay, Cerberus, plug in the Proof Extractor in over there, across the room from Alberto."

Cerberus plugged and powered up the extractor as Ricky barricaded the door to stop anyone from entering unexpectedly. As Cerberus plugged the machine in, he could've sworn he noticed Alberto's eye twitch unnaturally towards him.

"Okay, done."

"Now flip the gold switch on the back."

With a slight hum, the machine started up. As it began to softly glow and pulse, across the room, Alberto began to twitch. Maybe the machine had disturbed something buried deep inside him. Maybe the energy had been waiting—just waiting—for the right moment to surface. It almost seemed like the light in his skin was flickering, glowing in sync with the machine.

Ricky dimmed the lights. Alberto was definitely glowing now.

"Catch!"

Ricky tossed a proof-collection canister to Cerberus.

"Okay, so what's going to happen is — come into the center of the room between Alberto and the machine. I'll go over the machine and start it up. It's basically a giant energy magnet. Once I pull out the proof, you're going to have to catch it in the canister as it crosses the room."

"Why do I have to be the one to catch it?" Cerberus panicked. "I don't even know what 'it' is!"

"I'm the only one who knows how to work the machine!" Ricky called back. "At any rate, it's almost fully charged-up now. Look at Alberto. The bunny energy is definitely surging in him."

Across the room, Alberto had started to shake, with a hazy force emanating off him, pulling him – as much as it could, given the straps—toward the extractor.

"What is this proof, anyway?" Cerberus yelled across the room over the growing hum of the machine.

"I don't know, I only know how to extract it!" Ricky yelled back. "Are you ready?"

"Yeah, I guess!"

Ricky flipped the switch on the extractor, which caused the wheel to spin rapidly, focusing the glow upward to condense at the front of the megaphone mouth. It looked white-hot. Light disappeared from the room leaving only Alberto and the megaphone glowing.

Alberto roared. It wasn't a regular roar, and it wasn't a roar that sounded quite like a bunny's roar, either. He turned bright gold, as the ghostly form of a bunny emerged from him. It flickered, translucent and shifting, like a mirage of fur and light. Cute at first, it began growing more ferocious and more mutated as it drew closer. Passing the light fixtures on the wall, the bulbs shattered, and the electronic devices nearby began to turn on and off their own accord.

The barricaded door rattled violently. One of the nurses on the other side had noticed the commotion, or felt the vibration, and decided that it might be a good time to check on Mr. Broccolini.

It was definitely *not* a good time.

Between the shaking door handle, the glowing extractor, and the bunny energy, which at this point, was practically explosive as it surged across the room, Cerberus did his best to hold the canister steady, ready to make the catch.

"I'm going to surge it! Get ready!" Ricky called, barely audible now. "Turn the canister on!"

On? On?! Nobody had said anything about needing to turn the canister on—and now was not the best time for a crash course in using new electronic devices. Cerberus held the device steady, bracing as the pulsating energy surged his way, while simultaneously looking for the power switch.

Ricky hit the gold switch and all the remaining glass in the room shattered as the surge pulsed out. The energy formerly known as bunny warped even further as its skin shed and eyes grew as it ripped across the room towards Cerberus. But as scary as it was, he held the canister fast.

Finally, his paw found the button, a small yellow button on the bottom of the device. As the surging, furious energy rushed towards him, Cerberus pressed it, and with a crack of energy, bolts of lightning flashed, wind whipped his fur around torrentially, and the canister whirred into action, sucking in all the energy around it. All sound and light disappeared, and with a final flash, it seemed for a moment that nothing existed at all.

***

"Mr. Broccolini, are you all right?"

Cerberus opened his eyes and looked around. The room had been destroyed, and the emergency lights were on now. The barricaded door had been broken open by the onsite fire department, and a pack of nurses were now at Alberto's side, confused, because even though the room was destroyed, he somehow looked much better than he had earlier.

"I feel better than ever! I don't know what these kiddens did, but whatever it was worked! I finally feel like me again. Thank you."

With newfound life, Alberto Broccolini smiled across the room warmly at Cerberus and Ricky as they dusted glass shards off their lab coats.

Cerberus looked at the canister in his arms. It was now full of a thick golden substance that could only be described as a bunny energy pudding swirl. Success!

As Ricky and Cerberus disconnected the machine and prepared to leave, a nurse approached them.

"We just got off the phone with Mr. Broccolini's family, and they're forever grateful that he's feeling healthy again. We've been trying everything to help him, but none of our doctors could figure out any solutions that worked. What did you do to heal him?"

"Unfortunately, that's a trade secret," Ricky replied. "But if it ever happens to anyone again, let us know and we'll send someone out to handle it as soon as possible. And don't worry, we'll send some folks over later to help repair the examination room. Sorry for all the damage."

"Let me at least get you two some cocoa," said the nurse. "After all, you've earned it."

How could Cerberus and Ricky say no to that?

8

Back at the ARL, Cerberus and Ricky threw away their empty cocoa cups and connected the canister to the new portal. While everything about the process reminded Cerberus of the night he lost both his father and Lupita, he wasn't afraid of revisiting it. He had never thought that finding his father could be possible, and now he was closer than ever.

Using a stray hair pulled from one of Leonidas's old lab coats as a sample, Ricky instructed the lab to search for any energy pulses that could possibly be a match. While they searched, Cerberus took a quick nap to recharge. Having a state-of-the-art lab also meant having state-of-the-art sleeping facilities, and Cerberus was feeling refreshed and hopeful in no time.

"You know," Ricky said as Cerberus rejoined him in the lab. "If the board reacts positively to the ducklings, we'll get their trust, and then we'll probably get so much funding that creating pretty much any animal we've ever wanted to see will be possible."

"We?" Cerberus was confused. He wasn't a scientist, just a creative tiger who had experienced severe life trauma and ended up becoming a student at the Culinary Academy as a result. Maybe he could've been a scientist once, but not anymore. That possibility ended a long time ago.

"Of course, *we*," Ricky wasn't taking any excuses. "If not for you and Leonidas, we wouldn't have this lab, or the science, or the inspiration. This place is more yours than it is mine. Whenever you're ready, it will be here for you, and we'll finally be able to build the future together. No matter how long it takes."

A voice over the intercom summoned Ricky and Cerberus back to the portal room.

"Does this mean they found my dad?" Cerberus asked.

"It means that our machines have found a signal matching Leonidas's energy," Ricky said. "Now that we have the signal, we'll use the modified bunny energy in place of MonFus, and we should be able to calibrate our portal to take you to wherever he first arrived after the monster took him. In theory, that is."

"But does that mean we'll alert the beast, and it may attack again?" Cerberus hesitated. "How will bunny energy replicate the MonFus? I'm afraid I don't understand this stuff as much as my dad did."

A piglet lab assistant picked up where Ricky had left off. "Well, we've been working on this for a while," she said, "What we're able to make isn't quite the same kind of portal, since we only have the bunny energy and aren't using MonFus. Using the signal we located for Leonidas, we've been able to modify and recalibrate the bunny energy so it should be able to work in place of MonFus, but it's imperfect and there's a chemical imbalance."

"And what does that mean?" Cerberus took a step back.

"It means that this portal will only be able to transfer matter in one direction," the piglet replied. "MonFus is the only known substance that can generate a portal that work seamlessly in both directions, so basically this portal here won't be able to bring anyone or anything out."

"But we can definitely send someone in," Ricky followed up with an awkward smile.

"And then what happens when I get to the other side?" Cerberus was confused. The idea was to rescue Leonidas, not travel to an unknown dimension with no hope of returning.

"Well, what we think is… if you can find your dad… maybe he can build a new portal to send both of you back again from the other side," Ricky said. "It seems like your dad's science was calculated completely accurately. The only thing that got in the way was the monster. So…"

Cerberus was catching on. "So, what I need to do is go through the portal, kill the monster, and find my dad. Then the schematics for his original portal should be able to function as originally planned…"

"And we'll be able to bring the two of you home."

"Won't he need MonFus for his portal to work, too?"

"Likely yes," Ricky said. "Hopefully he'll know how to find some."

Cerberus took a deep breath. Finally, an opportunity to change what had happened that night ten years ago had presented itself. The odds didn't seem too good, but what other way was there?

He stepped closer to the portal, breathing slowly.

The piglet threw down a lever and pushed a few buttons. Slowly, the bunny energy filled the portal frame, and with a crack of light, the doorway began to glow as it opened. But this glow wasn't purple like before; this portal glowed a deep red. And where the other portal had felt like a doorway, this one felt more like a tunnel, sucking the energy in the room in one direction.

"You need to go now."

The piglet lab assistant spoke with urgency.

"If we exhaust this bunny energy, we'll need to locate another source before we can power the portal again."

"Alright C," Ricky said, "it's now or maybe never. You can do this."

As the portal glowed, Cerberus was reminded of that night ten years ago, and how horrible it had been. His spine tingled in response. But a decade had passed, and while life hadn't been ideal, it had continued. This portal went to who knew where, or better yet, who knew *when*, and entering it was just as risky as it could be rewarding.

But moments like this didn't come often, and Cerberus knew better than to take it for granted. For ten years, he had longed to see his father again, and now that there was an opportunity to make it a reality, he knew he couldn't just let it go. It didn't matter what was on the other side of the red doorway, and it didn't matter that he was under-packed and underprepared in nearly every way. This was reckless. Insane, even. But if there was even the slightest chance his father was out there, waiting… he had to take it. Cerberus knew there was only one choice. And he was making it.

"See you when I get back."

He took a breath, stepped forward, and in a flash of red light, the portal swallowed him whole.

9

Back when he was a kidden, on the rare mornings when he had time before Leonidas was ready to take him to the ARL, Cerberus would sit on the floor of the family room and watch TV. Lucinda didn't share the same appreciation for screens, and after a couple episodes of whatever was on that morning, she would make Cerberus turn off the device and spend an hour playing outside to keep things balanced.

Cerberus was incredibly fascinated by the way that the TV would turn off when he pushed the little button in the corner. The image on the screen would quickly shrink and distort into a tiny, circular dot before vanishing into blackness with a pop. It was captivating. Where did the show go? Why did it have to shrink out of view, twisting into a new shape before it could go away completely?

Entering the red portal felt exactly as Cerberus had always imagined all those TV shows felt when he had turned the screen off, sending them through their own portal back to wherever they had been broadcast from. As he journeyed through the portal, he felt shrunken, stretched, and quite possibly pulled inside out. Light and color flashed, distorted into strange shapes around and through him, and he could swear he saw flashing echoes of the monster flickering in and out around him as well.

For a moment, Cerberus was threaded through total blackness, which shifted into a circular planet that felt to be part of a familiar, yet unusual, solar system. The planets were eyes, which floated around him, forming the face of a giant basset hound. The hound's nose dripped, and instantly everything morphed again, flowing like liquid, which generated plains and woods around him as it settled. As a sky formed, Cerberus could see a haunting light touch the land that was solidifying around him. It looked familiar, but also different in a strange, way he couldn't quite put his paw on. It was as though he was standing in the same spot in which he had stood before he entered the portal, yet also he felt as though he was somewhere else entirely at the same time.

In a far off, translucent distance, Cerberus could see Dot and the Culinary Academy. He could see Henry and Lucinda driving across the country. He saw Leonidas pinning up one of his drawings of an imagined giraffe, from when he had been a much younger kidden. He saw the ruins he had passed on his way to the Culinary Academy, but they now strangely looked much less ruined than they had when he had last seen them.

A sun flashed into the sky and began to cycle backwards, slowly at first, and then so quickly it became a strobing flicker. The earth rumbled as the surrounding ruins pulled themselves out of the ground, the covering vines receded into their seeds and vanished, and buildings rose back out of the earth. Tall trees rose out of the dust, and Cerberus fell out the sky towards them—but just before impact, he snapped back up, shrank down to a pop much like the TV turning off, and was gone.

10

Cerberus opened his eyes. The sun was rising over a beautiful river, and as he stood up to take in his surroundings, he realized he was sleeping under a grove of pine trees. Was this the portal dimension? Where was he? Where should he go next?

He splashed some water on his face, and began walking, following the channel as he explored the area. Was he the only one here? It didn't seem like there was any civilization nearby, at least not that he could sense. Reaching a cliff, the river broke into a waterfall, and Cerberus looked out over the surrounding valley. In the distance, he could see a few smoke plumes rising through the trees. Fire generally meant civilization, and maybe somebody over there would be able to point him in a good direction.

Cerberus found a narrow path and descended the cliff carefully. He could tell that this wasn't going to be a quick journey, and after walking for several hours, the sun began to dip, and night started to set in. Cerberus hadn't been outside, on his own in the dark in a very long time and could preemptively feel his spine starting to tingle. He knew that traveling though the portal had brought him closer to the monster, and he was going to have to do something to keep himself safe as he settled into this new environment, lest the monster catch him before he was ready.

First things first, he would need a new fire. Cerberus experimented with grinding various stones against each other as he walked, and finally came across a rusted piece of steel that created a little shower of sparks when he smashed a rock against it.

"Nice work, little one." Cerberus could imagine Leonidas's satisfaction of watching this experiment pay off.

Reaching a clearing as the sun continued to set, Cerberus built himself a camp using a sturdy tree as a central post. He wrapped wood and twigs with river reeds, and now armed with several torches, lined the area, creating a warm wall of glowing safety. When he was finally finished, he climbed up into the tree, where he lay down to conceal himself atop a sturdy leaf canopy, ready for the night to come. He would wait until morning came before he would sleep; it was probably smarter to stay up tonight to observe.

The sun finally disappeared from the sky, and a light green haze hovered over the oncoming darkness. Cerberus sat up in his tree and watched. Soon, he felt the familiar tingle and could hear breathing through the trees. Branches buckled as a monstrous, shadowy form slithered through them, and soon enough, Cerberus could faintly see the pairs of blue eyes watching him, glowing enough to see the beast's two mouths, each fixed into a knowingly sly smile.

The fur stood up further on Cerberus's back than it ever had. Sure, at home, he had had felt something like this feeling every night, but tonight was so much stronger. It felt as though his spine was about to burst into flames, and Cerberus's eyes darted down, checking the torches he had lit around him, wishing with all his might that no strong gusts of wind blew through until the crack of dawn.

But the beast never did approach the fire barrier, as Cerberus knew—well, hoped—it wouldn't, and after watching the tiger for a while, the eyes finally dimmed, satisfied, and the shadowy form slithered away again through the trees. Cerberus watched the treetops shake as it disappeared until it was far out of sight, and he could no longer hear the crunching of leaves.

He was alone now. The tingle calmed, but he spent the night awake anyway. Just in case it came back again. It didn't.

11

As the sun rose the following morning, Cerberus climbed down from his tree, extinguished his torches, and strapped a few together to carry on his back. Cautiously, he made his way out to from where the beast had been watching and could clearly a trail of smashed trees and dragged ground left in its wake. This was real, not his imagination – even if he wished it was. The last time he'd seen physical evidence of the monster was when it took Leonidas, so he must be on the right path. But that last time had been on accident. This time it was on purpose. Finding the monster was the whole point of this journey, and as scary and reckless as it felt, he knew this was the path he had to follow.

As Cerberus walked along the beast's trail, he observed that the woods weren't just regular woods, but plants growing over other ruins of past destruction. Bits of metal and plastic poked through the ground and trees along the way; nothing very noticeable, but certainly not nature in its purest form. Cerberus wondered what could've been here before, and what had happened for it to become like this. Tripping over a rock, Cerberus realized it was a container, covered in layers of moss and sand. A petrified canister, the perfect canteen. It might not be clean, it certainly wasn't, but there weren't many other options here. Luckily, the familiar forked stream still followed the path of the monster. Cerberus dipped his new, slightly used, canteen into the crisp flow, filling it with questionable, yet cold, water.

***

Finally, after about six or seven days—as best as Cerberus could keep track, given his increasing delirium due to hunger—he spotted smoke rising above the trees.

Smoke meant fire. Fire often meant civilization. But would this be the kind of civilization who welcomed strangers—or the kind who made them disappear?

Cautiously, he followed the smoke, veering off the beast's trail and soon found a small village consisting of huts, storehouses, community spaces, and even a large water tower, all entirely constructed from crushed metallic bricks and plastic. Whoever lived here must have pulled the materials up out of the ruins embedded in the surrounding land to build with.

Even from the border, Cerberus could tell that this village lacked the technology he had back home. No streetlights, power-sidewalks, or automatic doors; this place seemed like it didn't have anything that used electricity at all. It felt almost as if the village existed in a completely different universe than his own. He wondered if any larger cities in the region would be like this too, or if this village was the exception. Cerberus made a mental note not to talk about too many things from back home, as he didn't want to draw any attention that he didn't have to.

At the center of this community stood a large, roaring bonfire, kept alive by several deer and raccoon folk who stockpiled wood, clearly gathered from the nearby forest. The fire was bright enough to feel the heat at the edge of the farthest building and judging by the fact that the monster's trail curved around the village, avoiding it completely, Cerberus knew that this fire did more than simply keep the citizens here warm during cold nights.

All eyes were on Cerberus as he approached. Given what he'd been through, he knew he must look terrible. A few mothers hurried out of their homes, anxious to keep a careful eye on their kiddens who played nearby, as he, the stranger, stepped paw after paw into their domain. A few confident citizens even covered their noses. Cerberus didn't take it personally; he knew he smelled bad, too. The fire was warm, and quickly the heat made him very aware of just how hungry he was. A week without proper food wasn't easy for anyone to handle, especially someone with a degree in the culinary arts.

Cerberus stumbled in his stupor, and while things were indeed getting a bit hazy, he could make out a large figure with what seemed like enormous antlers approaching him. Cerberus fell to his knees, but a hoof caught his paw and helped him back up.

"Can someone come'n get this cubbin some food? He looks skinnier than a carnivore in a cabbage patch!"

With a deep, heavy laugh, another figure approached, and together, the two helped Cerberus make his way into one of the nearby huts.

"Don't you worry, we're gonna come fix you right up."

Cerberus collapsed onto a bed, which was incredibly comfortable. Soon a wet towel had been placed over his forehead, and a hot bowl of soup had been shoved between his paws. It didn't matter if the chef had been professionally trained or not—the food was delicious.

Though Cerberus started with a spoon, he quickly moved to lapping it up with his tongue, and finally caved to drinking the broth from the bowl as if it was water. Warm friendly voices laughed around him, and as he finished licking the bowl clean, he looked up, and the fuzzy figures came back into focus as the nutrients made their way through his body.

"There ya go, cubbin, that should be doing the trick for ya. Had us scared for a minute there, ya did."

At the center of the room, looking down at him, a massive buck stood, dressed in a beautiful golden robe. He smiled down warmly at Cerberus, extending his hoof again. Cerberus shook it with his paw.

"The name's Johnsto. Welcome to the village, cubbin. Now whereabouts are ya comin' from?"

From nearby, a doe, busy tightening a beautifully crafted dress on her daughter called, "Come on, Johnsto, look at his state. Give him a minute to recover."

"Okay, Clora, you're right, you're right." Johnsto grabbed some new robes out of a pile and tossed them over to Cerberus. "Get these robes on, they breathe well. You'll be passing out in near under a second unless you change into something lighter."

Cerberus looked around at the many curious faces staring at this new visitor. Did they all expect him to change right in front of them?

"Just go through to the little room in the back." Johnsto threw his head back with a heavy laugh. "You can keep your stuff there. It's nearly night, so we'll set up a bed for ya. You can stay one day or even twenty, we're welcoming folk here. And once you're feeling strong again, I'll take you around and show you the village."

Cerberus stuttered. "I can't stay here for the night. The monster…"

Johnsto just laughed again, as he wrapped his arm around Cerberus's shoulder in a firm, confident, yet warm grip.

"There are no monsters here at night, cubbin, that's what the fire is for. Now never you worry, we'll be safe."

With a little assistance, Cerberus made it to the back room, changed into his new clothing. Instantly, he felt much better, and the faint feelings faded away as cool air set in. These robes really did breathe well in the heat. He thought about what Johnsto kept calling him. *Cubbin*. It felt like it was similar in meaning to *kidden*, which he had always been called back home in his youth, but it also felt warmer, cozier. But maybe that's just because Johnsto was saying it, and he had that energy that made you feel comfortable and welcome with just a single look. This wasn't Cerberus's home sure, but it was the closest he had felt to being in one in a long time. It was different, but good different. If that meant anything. He wondered what else was different here.

Clora and Johnsto brought more water, as well as some snacks, and set them by the bedside. Clora caught Cerberus's turning away from the glow of the fire creeping under the windows.

"Sorry it's so bright for your sleeping, but you know how it is with monsters and darkness, all that."

"No, this is perfect."

"One last thing—what's your name, cubbin? Can't just be calling you 'cubbin' all the time."

"Cerberus."

"Well, it's good to have you, Cerberus," Johnsto said warmly.

"It's good to be here, Johnsto," Cerberus mumbled, already halfway asleep. "You don't know how good it is to be here."

And with that, Cerberus drifted off to sleep.

12

Cerberus woke the following morning feeling more rested than he had in years. The clothing that Johnsto had provided fit great, and from his bed, Cerberus watched some young cubbins play gleefully with his old clothing in the main room.

After taking in his surroundings as much as was possible from his bedside, Cerberus made his way into the main room of Johnsto's home, where Clora and a few other folks he hadn't met yet were crafting a meal. Clora beckoned for Cerberus to join them, and once he sat down, she called the cubbins over and introduced him to everyone.

"Cubbins, this is Cerberus. He's a traveler who will be staying with us for a few nights," Clora said as they gathered, eyes wide at the sight of someone so unfamiliar. "Cerberus, these fine cubbins you see before you are Burtie, Garlack, Philop, and Northsie."

"Where are you traveling from?" Northsie asked.

"I'm not really sure," Cerberus replied.

"Well, where are you going?" Northsie asked.

"I'm not really sure," Cerberus replied.

"Come, Cerberus needs to eat," Clora said, taking his paw. "Please join us for lunch."

As the group shared fresh bread, soup, and jerky, Clora explained that this was the town of Bismarthi, and that they were about two hundred and fifty miles away from the closest kingdom, Cathorn. Bismarthi had a population of about seventy-five, and was a very tight-knight, close community. The citizens of Bismarthi took pride in their empathy; it was a place where everyone shared their skills; chipping in to support and help each other as much as possible to help ensure that every citizen in the town was able to live as happy and healthy of a life as they could.

Bismarthi had been started by Johnsto' s grandfather, Alaine, who was originally from Cathorn, but as the stories go, eventually decided he wanted to find his own land to establish a new community with a unique sense of values compared to those expected of the Cathornese citizens. So, he and several good friends packed up their buffalo-driven wagons and embarked with their families into the depths of the forest, in search of the perfect spot to start their lives anew.

Together, they founded Bismarthi; by building the first community center, using reclaimed material like plastic, rubber, steel, and aluminum they dug up from the Earth, and the town quickly took off on its own from there. In its present-day form, Bismarthi now boasted several large family homes, cozy cottages, a meat-storage facility, a water tower, a small schoolhouse, a grain depot, a blacksmith, a tailor's shop, and a community bonfire that was fed constantly as to never burn out. Just outside of town, and safe from the heat of the bonfire, were the Bismarthi fields and farm, where citizens grew vegetables, wheat, and even the thin reed fibers they used for their heat-friendly clothing. Johnsto was over there now, tending to the crops, as it was his day to do so according to the community chore wheel. He'd be back soon, and Clora promised that if Cerberus was up for it, Johnsto would be more than excited to show him around.

"Oh, I would love to see everything!" Cerberus replied enthusiastically, through a mouthful of jerky and granola.

So, when Johnsto came home from a morning of farming and had changed into some more comfortable day wear, he took Cerberus out to see it all. Walking along the circular path that separated the town from the large, well-tended bonfire in the center, Cerberus noticed that Johnsto barely broke a sweat. The folks in Bismarthi were much more used to being next to a giant fire than he was. Even more interestingly, Cerberus realized that of all the folks he had seen in this town, none of them looked like the folks he knew back home. Antlers, thick fur, big eyes, and bushy tails spanned the population; everyone looked naturally inclined to not only withstand, but thrive in the local weather and ecosystems, at least much more than he was.

As they passed the schoolhouse, Cerberus noticed a large squirrel, also in a flashy robe, teaching a pack of cubbins who answered his questions both eagerly and accurately. Passing the tailor and blacksmith, Cerberus was impressed to see just how much a small group of motivated, happy villagers could accomplish. Though nothing was particularly fancy, the citizens of Bismarthi were hardly living in poverty; everyone had what they needed and more.

"So are you, like, the mayor here?" Cerberus asked Johnsto, trying to see more of the bigger picture.

Johnsto laughed and slapped Cerberus on the back with his hoof warmly. "I don't know what a *mayor* is cubbin, but I can tell you that there isn't any leader here in Bismarthi. We were started by a group, and so we always do what's best for the group. I look out for everyone, the same as everyone looks out for me. If you're here, we'll look out for you, and we expect you to also look out for us in return."

"Clora said you were out on the farm this morning. Do you work there every day?"

"No, we distribute community tasks by using our chore wheel. It makes sure we're all dividing the work amongst ourselves fairly. When our cubbins become old enough to participate, we have a Choring-of-Age ceremony, where we add their name to the wheel— and then we watch them proudly accomplish their first set of chores. If you're planning on staying, we'll add you to the chore wheel as well. Do you think you will? You're more than welcome to make a life for yourself here among all of us."

Things seemed so much simpler here in Bismarthi, and for a moment, Cerberus truly did wish that he could stay, add his name to the chore wheel, and become a true member of this supportive community. But of course, he couldn't. That wasn't why he'd come all this way. He needed to find his father and couldn't afford to spend his time amidst these distractions while on such an important adventure.

"Thank you so much for taking care of me, and while I would love to stay here, I'm just passing through." Cerberus felt better as he reminded himself of his goals. "I'm on a mission to locate my father, so once I'm fully back on my feet, I'll need to keep moving."

"Locate your father? Is he missing?" Johnsto frowned, concerned. "Do you have any idea where he might be?"

"I don't know. I don't even really know where I am."

Johnsto stopped walking, causing Cerberus to accidentally bump into him. Together, they stood at the edge of the town.

"Well then, how do you expect to find him?"

Solemnly, Cerberus looked ahead. From where he stood, he could see the trail of the beast, a dragged groove in the earth wrapped around the far edge town, as far from the bonfire, disappearing into the woods several hundred feet away.

"I know what took him."

"The two-headed dragon."

From Johnsto's expression, Cerberus could tell he understood.

"We don't know much about the beast, but long ago, when Bismarthi was being established, the two-headed dragon found us one night," Johnsto said. "It attacked, trying to raid us, until my father waved a torch towards it, and it retreated— so the following morning that, we built our bonfire. Since then, we've kept it burning day and night, and because of it the dragon has stayed at bay."

"Do you have any idea why wishes to attack you? Where it comes from? Do you have a portal somewhere around here, too?" Cerberus was full of questions. "Sometimes I feel it watching me from the shadows, almost like a haunting spirit, but I've only seen it in the flesh twice—once when it took my dad, and then again when I arrived here."

Johnsto sighed. "Sadly, cubbin, I don't know the answers to your questions. And I don't know what a 'portal' is. But what I can tell you is this, if you follow the dragons trail, it will lead you to Cathorn, the only place that doesn't keep a fire burning."

"Do you think it has to do with why your grandfather left?"

"I don't know the exact reasons my grandfather had when he left, but I do know Cathorn is a place of darkness, and that the two-headed dragon always heads in its direction after a victorious hunt."

"Then I need to go to Cathorn. Any hope of finding my dad will be there."

Cerberus strained his eyes as he looked down the trail ahead. Cathorn must be far away. Though he could see the horizon, he couldn't make out any kingdoms, even faintly.

"Do you think I might be able to borrow some supplies? I really shouldn't stay here much longer."

Johnsto turned and started walking towards his home, beckoning for Cerberus to follow.

"Look here, cubbin. We're a supportive community here in Bismarthi and will do what we can to help you on your journey. However, you're weak now. Without help, you won't survive the journey to Cathorn. Stay with us for a couple more nights, gain your strength back, help us with our chores, and in turn, let us help you prepare for your journey. Our dear cubbin Northsie, who you met this morning, is having her Choring-of-Age in two nights' time. Join us in celebration, and then we'll see you off on your journey, healthy and ready to fight for your father."

"You think I'll have to fight?"

"To retrieve something taken by the two-headed dragon? I've never done it myself, but I can't imagine any other way," Johnsto smiled. "Now, let's head to the blacksmith. For the rest of my chores today, I'm scheduled to work on forging steel rivets to fix the supports on the water tower. If you're willing to help me out, maybe we can make you some tools while we're over there, too."

So, Cerberus and Johnsto spent the next few hours in the smithy. Cerberus pumped the bellows to heat the steel that Dinna and Parlie had dug up from the ruins, and Johnsto used a heavy anvil and hammer to pound the molten rivets flat. As the new rivets and bolts cooled in a tub of water, Johnsto melted some extra steel to fashion a large knife for Cerberus.

Working in the smithy with Johnsto, Cerberus couldn't help but remember back when he used to build, invent, and imagine with his father back home. Though he had never stopped making and imagining, he couldn't remember the last time he had really worked this closely with someone else since back then. After the accident, he thought he never would again, yet here he was, on the other side of a mysterious portal in a completely unfamiliar town, working hand in hand with another passionate, smart, and inspiring leader. He watched as Johnsto poured the molten steel into a flat mold, feeling a sense of childlike wonder and excitement to see what would happen next.

"Do you like traveling? Or do you miss your home?"

Cerberus hadn't noticed that Northsie had wandered over as well, still curious about him, the stranger.

"I do miss my home," said Cerberus. "But I also like traveling, because each step means I'm getting closer to returning to my home once again."

"I'd like to go traveling," Northsie said. "But my parents want me to stay here, in Bismarthi. They say the rest of the world is too dangerous, and I'm too young."

"When I was your age, I thought the same thing," Cerberus said. "But now that I'm older, I realize that if you have something special, you should do everything you can to take care of it."

"Maybe taking care of something means letting it do what it needs to do, even if it's not what you want it to do."

This was an unusually wise thing for a cubbin to say, but before Cerberus could think of a response, Northsie was already off, running down the path towards Garlack and Burtie who tossed her a ball, initiating some sort of game.

"Hey Cubbin!" Johnsto called. "We'll have to finish up your knife later, the rivets are ready. Time to get them up on the tower."

With the help of Dinna, Johnsto climbed up the water tower to attach them to the base and the pipes for reinforcement. Cerberus offered to lend a paw as well, but Johnsto cautioned that *"Some chores require more experience than others,"* and sent him off to help Clora, who was back in the main hut cutting, tanning, and stretching leather.

Together, Cerberus and Clora pulled and sewed the leather straps needed to make strong work gloves for Northsie, who would be needing some for her daily chores once her Choring-of-Age celebration was over. Clora helped Cerberus stretch some extra leather straps so he could sew some gloves of his own; but then a bell rang, and Galletta called everyone for dinner, so that set of gloves would have to wait to be finished later.

"We'll have to make you a new canteen as well. That petrified thing you're using can't be sanitary."

Clora added it to the list of chores on the wheel, directly under *Teach Nan to fish*.

The townsfolk of Bismarthi gathered near the bonfire, excited to partake in the dinner that Galletta had spent the day preparing. Delicious soup, bread, and buffalo jerky were passed around and happily shared by all. Though he remained cautious out of instinct, Cerberus took in the serenity of his surroundings as he finished his meal.

"I wish you could stay longer."

Cerberus turned to see Northsie back at his side, looking up at him.

"Yeah," added Petablo. "You'd love my salad and risotto, but it's not my turn to cook dinner until next week."

"I'll have to try it next time I visit."

After dinner and a few songs, the sun was nearly set. Parlie, Jacoby, and Nan stayed up, as it was their turn to keep watch as the rest of the villagers headed back to their homes. As Cerberus changed from his daytime clothes into his new sleep robes and climbed into his cozy, but temporary, bed, he couldn't help but wish for a moment that he could forget his troubles ahead and make a life for himself here in Bismarthi. He could see the pride that each citizen took in their daily accomplishments. It would be a true honor to be added to the community chore wheel. He really did want to try Petablo's risotto, and he would love an opportunity to share his culinary skills in return—but tomorrow night was Northsie's Choring-of-Age, and then the following morning, he'd say his goodbyes and continue making his way to Cathorn. He had made it this far, and he couldn't possibly give up now.

As Cerberus drifted off to sleep, not even the tingle bothered him. It was an all too rare, yet very much needed, moment of piece.

13

Early the following morning, Cerberus joined Clora and Galletta at the farm to help sow seeds for crops and harvest the fabric that had matured and was finally ripe for picking and processing.

As the three led the buffalo-driven plows through the field, planting popcorn, wheat, vegetable, and silk seeds, Clora explained that the reason the farm wasn't located close to the fire like the rest of the village was because the heat from the fire wouldn't allow things to grow properly. For this reason, they only visited the farm during the day, and if a chore wasn't completed by early evening, they would return to the village and wait until the following morning to complete it. It wasn't safe to be this far away once night fell.

Cerberus was fascinated by how the silky fabric grew, with individual bunches growing off the sprout, blowing in the wind like luxurious, flowing hair. Cerberus held the sprouts as Galletta and Clora pulled the strands, taking each batch through a comb to untangle any messes as they spooled it up. As part of his weekly chores, Massimo was scheduled to do tailoring tomorrow, so he'd be the one responsible for weaving the fabric into the wonderfully breathable clothing that Cerberus had come to deeply appreciate.

In honor of the occasion, all chores were scheduled to end early today, so that everyone could participate in celebrating Northsie's Choring-of-Age, and since Cerberus wasn't knowledgeable enough in the traditions of Bismarthi, he was given a few hours off even earlier as everyone else went about finishing up their festival-specific chores.

Cerberus gathered his unfinished leather straps, some thread, a few strips of steel, his unfinished dull knife, and a sharpening stone. Then he climbed up to the top of the water tower to sit and work on his new tools. After attempting to sew gloves for the first time with no experience proved unsuccessful, he decided he could just wrap the leather straps around his paws for temporary protection and went to work on sharpening his new knife instead.

As Cerberus ran the dull blade back and forth against the sharpening stone, he stared out in the direction of Cathorn, squinting his eyes as best as he could in a hopeful effort to make out any blurry castles or kingdoms on the horizon. While he could see a couple of smoke pillars in the distance, which likely marked the locations of a few other villages, everything eventually disappeared into the distance, and nothing could be seen further than that. Cathorn seemed like it might even be farther away than Johnsto had said, and he would just have to follow the two-headed dragon's trail and trust that it would lead him there. Cerberus thought about asking Johnsto if he might be able to borrow a buffalo-driven cart. Even though he was feeling much better, making that distance on foot seemed close to impossible.

Cerberus's focus on knife sharpening and horizon watching was broken by warm sounds of cheerful live music staring from down below, and he realized the Choring-of-Age must be starting. Carefully, with an extra leather strap, he secured his knife to his side and climbed down from the water tower. At the bottom, he found Jacoby and Petablo, and together they all walked over towards the bonfire to join the ceremony.

A stage had been set up, where Northsie stood proudly with her parents closely behind her. After the crowd had gathered, the music died down, and Johnsto took the stage, wearing magnificent golden robes. His antlers had been wrapped in gold for the occasion, and with the sun reflecting off him on one side and the fire reflecting off the other, he shined almost like a star.

"Friends and family of Bismarthi!" Johnsto called out to the crowd. "Today we celebrate the Choring-of-Age of cubbin Northsie, who officially begins her adult life as a contributor to the community in Bismarthi by having her name added to our daily chore wheel."

Johnsto leaned down as to be face to face with Northsie.

"Northsie, I am honored that my assigned chore today is to present you with your first chore."

Johnsto reached into his robe and pulled out a small steel plaque with *Northsie* carved into it. "This plaque, imprinted with your name represents your place in our community as an adult. I am proud to declare that your first chore will be to add it to our community chore wheel—so that you may join our community in supporting and caring for each other, through the completion of various daily chores."

The crowd cheered as Parlie and Clora rolled the chore wheel up onto the stage.

"Northsie, take your plaque, and place it on the chore wheel."

Slowly and carefully, Northsie approached the chore wheel, and pressed the plaque into the place that had been carved to hold it. As she stepped back, Johnsto raised a large hammer and confidently pounded the plaque in firmly.

The crowd cheered with each *clang* from the hammer. Northsie looked out at her fellow supportive adults and smiling parents. A giant grin spread across her face.

"Now spin the wheel, Northsie," Johnsto called out, "and let's see what your first official community chore tomorrow will be."

With a deep breath, Northsie spun the giant arrow affixed to the middle of the chore wheel. The arrow spun, quickly at first, passing various chores, until it finally slowed down and landed on *building repair*. The crowd roared in celebration.

"Northsie! Tomorrow at sunrise, your first chore will be to examine the buildings of Bismarthi to check for necessary repairs." Johnsto called out. "Finding any damage and making the repairs will help keep our buildings standing and our homes safe. It is a very important chore indeed."

Through more cheers, Northsie's parents revealed a beautiful new robe that had been fashioned by Massimo for Northsie. Lined with stunning colors woven through the fabric, the garment was a perfect fit. With pride beaming from her face, Northsie stepped forward to address the crowd.

"Everyone!" Northsie called out, as the crowd hushed. "I am so honored to be a part of this community and even more honored to finally place my name on the chore wheel alongside all of the folks I admire. I will do my best to make the community of Bismarthi proud, doing my daily chores as best as I can so that we may continue to grow and prosper."

Cerberus had never seen so many folks who were excited about doing chores. He remembered being a kidden back home, complaining when Lucinda had asked something as simple as for him to take out the trash. Things were different here, and the natural enthusiasm and positivity shared by all made the idea of chores seem much nicer than it had to Cerberus in the past. Cerberus noted that if he ever made it back home, he would try to bring these positive traits of enthusiasm about community collaboration towards completion of chores along with him.

Gathering in a circle, everyone passed bowls of food around, and the Choring-of-Age feast began. Music and singing began as everyone ate, and soon, half of the citizens of Bismarthi had abandoned their food in favor of dancing. They formed a circle around Northsie, who broke into a dance that had clearly been rehearsed. Either that, or she was just a natural.

Even for someone with a degree in the culinary arts, this meal was impressive. Finishing his second bowl, Cerberus made his way through the crowd over to Johnsto and Clora. Johnsto pulled him into a joyous dance.

"Cubbin! Are you enjoying yourself? I do hope so! Not every passing traveler is lucky enough to attend a festival like this!"

Cerberus could barely keep up with Johnsto's moves but nevertheless tried his best to follow along.

"Johnsto, I was hoping I might be able to borrow a cart for the Journey tomorrow to Cathorn. Might there be one you could spare?"

Johnsto stop dancing. Sitting down on a nearby stool, he beckoned for Cerberus to join him.

"I'll be honest with you Cerberus, even if your father is still alive, the odds of finding him, defeating the two-headed dragon, and escaping in one piece are extremely slim," Johnsto sighed. "I should know; my grandfather almost didn't make it out of Cathorn. He traveled this far away before stopping to establish Bismarthi for a reason. And you're welcome to stay with us here, should you choose. Everyone loves you, you've done your chores well, and I have to say—"

"I understand, Johnsto. And I thank you for both your hospitality and your concern," Cerberus said, "but for me, staying here in Bismarthi isn't an option. I don't only owe it to my father, there are many others back home who are counting on me to do my best and not give up. I can't just stop now; I know in my heart I must try."

Johnsto put his arm over Cerberus's shoulders, and gave him a firm, supportive squeeze.

"I have to tell you, even if you think you understand what you're up against, you don't." Johnsto looked back out at the crowd celebrating around Northsie around the bonfire. "But we're a supportive community, and no matter what happens we will support you and your decisions as best we can."

"I do wish I could stay too. I wish I was here under a different circumstance," Cerberus said. "But look at Northsie. She is so excited to do her chores and make her community proud. This mission is my chore, and I need to complete it to make my community proud. Thank you for your hospitality and welcoming me in, but I can't give up now."

Johnsto understood.

"Clora and I will pack you some supplies, and as soon as the sun comes up, we'll see you off with one of our strongest and most durable carts. But don't forget, you'll always be welcome here in Bismarthi."

Noticing the serious conversation, Clora pulled both the tiger and the buck up from their seats.

"But you're not leaving yet," Clora smiled. "So let's get back out there and enjoy the party. One more night of peace together."

So, they did. More food flowed, while laughter and music filled the air. After a few hours folks began to tire out, retreating to their homes one by one for some well-deserved sleep.

Cerberus, Johnsto, Pippin, Catalina, and Northsie were some of the last few awake, and once most folks had gone to bed, they quieted down and shared a few stories around the fire. Pippin was a more recent addition to the Bismarthi population, having moved from the village of Grendail, forming a strong alliance between the two communities. Catalina had big dreams of building her own boat and sailing it down the river with her family one day, perhaps to establish a new city of her own. This inspired Johnsto to tell the story of how his grandfather had picked the land on which he founded Bismarthi. The soil was full of nutrients, and there were plenty of trees and found materials for burning in the large fire, without negatively affecting the ecosystem. Cerberus thought about sharing some stories of his youth, but the world he came from seemed too confusing to explain at this hour, so he decided that those were stories for another time.

Finally, Northsie nodded off to sleep, so Catalina carried her home to bed. Everyone else took that as a cue to head to bed as well.

As Cerberus settled into his bed for one final night's sleep in Bismarthi, he made a promise to himself that if his mission went according to plan, he'd stop by one more time on the way home to say goodbye. He really did like it here.

14

Cerberus awoke suddenly and looked around. He could swear he had just heard something. Something loud. Was it a creak? Or was it a roar? Through his window, he could see the light of the fire flickering. Maybe it was nothing.

Cerberus shut his eyes.

There it was again, only louder this time. Yells followed.

The tiger leapt out of bed, grabbed his bag, threw on his clothes, and ran outside to find Johnsto, Parlie, Jacoby, and Galletta throwing leather ropes around the water tower, pulling to provide additional suspension as it continued to bend at a strange angle. Johnsto yelled for everyone to pull, and everyone stepped back together, pulling the leather straps, countering the tilting water tower.

"What happened?" Cerberus ran over. His paws wrapped in his own leather straps to protect them, he pulled at the additional supports on the collapsing tower as hard as he could.

"The new rivets weren't strong enough!" Johnsto called. "The heat from the bonfire had damaged the structural integrity much more than we realized. Pull, everyone! We must stop the tower from collapsing!"

The tower groaned and lurched forward as one of the legs buckled and bent under its weight.

"What's going on?"

"Is the water tower going to fall?"

The chaos had awoken more of the citizens of Bismarthi, and a crowd was gathering. Massimo ran from the tailor shop, carrying more leather straps. As Johnsto, Cerberus, and the others pulled the tower back, Massimo wrapped the additional straps around the tower legs and pulled as well.

By now everyone was outside, including Northsie, who was still dressed in her new Choring-of-Age robe. As the newest adult in Bismarthi, she looked to find a way to help.

"We need to drain the water tower! It's too heavy!"

With full confidence, Northsie ran under the tower and threw her weight against the warped latch that was keeping a drainage faucet sealed. The latch gave way at once and the faucet cap burst open, releasing a flood of water. Northsie flew back, caught safely in the arms of her parents. Everyone looked up at the tower as the pressure relaxed and it began to settle back into place as the water drained out.

After a moment of bated breath, the tower was once again stable. Braving the gushing pipe, Johnsto pushed the cap down over the flowing water and sealed the latch. Everyone held their breath as they waited to see what would happen next.

"You see, everyone?" Johnsto called out. "This is why it is important to learn the value of chores!"

The community erupted into a thunderous cheer as everyone praised Northsie in celebration of her quick thinking and success. But suddenly, and without warning the earth emanated a low, deep, reverberating hum, as a powerful vibration rippled across its surface and throughout Bismarthi. The water tower began to shake, the hum echoing up the legs and through the tank. The cheering silenced, and stopping their celebration, everyone listened closely as the hum grew louder, and louder. Very quickly, the vibrations turned into violent shakes.

"Earthquake!"

Everyone scrambled to find safety as nearby structures shook and the glass on the windows shattered.

"Hold the tower steady. This will pass!"

Johnsto and the others resumed pulling on the leather straps to help support the tower, but due to the shaking ground, they were unable to hold their footing. Falling and tumbling into the muddy water under the tower that had gathered from the pressure release, the leather straps whipped out of their paws and swung around in a giant tangle.

The structure groaned and heaved as the final rivets snapped off, releasing the massive tank at the top. Everyone watched as it rocked back and forth, finally tumbling down towards the ground as the tower's legs gave way under the weight.

"Run!"

Nobody had to be told twice, and as the citizens of Bismarthi ducked for cover, Cerberus watched the tank explode on impact, releasing a huge flood into the streets. Contained between buildings, the wave pushed towards the town center, where it extinguished the massive bonfire instantly.

Bismarthi went dark.

The earth groaned and shook again.

A voice that sounded like Johnsto's called out through the darkness. "Everyone, get back to your homes now!"

Everyone did the best they could to wade through the mud and darkness in the hope of find their homes.

"Don't worry, I'll help you!" A small hoof grabbed Cerberus's paw, and he realized it must belong to Northsie. Basically blind, he followed her, stumbling through the streets.

"You need to get back to your parents!" Cerberus called out to the small figure shrouded in darkness in front of him. "They're going to be worried!"

"No!" Northsie called back. "I'm an adult now, and I need to help support my community!"

As they ran, voices sounded in the background as various folks struggled to relight the soaked firewood. Across the area, a few small torches flickered alight in various homes.

The earth vibrated again, and a cold breeze moved through the town, carried by a shadow. Cerberus fell in pain. His spine had never tingled this much. Writhing in the mud, he squinted through the smoke and darkness to make out the figures around him.

"Cerberus? Cerberus?" Somewhere in the darkness, Northsie called out.

Slowly, one of figures came into view.

"Northsie, is that you?" Cerberus could barely see more than a shape in the darkness approaching. He struggled against the discomfort in his spine, fighting to stand up.

The figure approaching him began to rise, a large plume of smoke and ash dragging behind it. This was not Northsie—it was something massive, and as Cerberus's eyes continued to adjust to the darkness, the towering figure settled into its form, its silhouette appearing against the moon behind it. Cerberus stumbled back, slipping into the mud once again as it leaned forward through the smoke.

"Cerberus?" Northsie called again.

"Northsie, get out of here now!"

Cerberus yelled as the silhouette snapped alert, and with a roar that shook the streets, two bright blue eyes began to glow. Even though it was just a story to many, a fairy tale even, there was no doubt that they were in the presence of the two-headed dragon.

Johnsto looked up, dropping his flint, which was instantly lost in the mud surrounding the wet ruins of the bonfire. Everyone scattered as the dragon plunged, in hot pursuit of Johnsto as he ran. With his antlers still wrapped in gold, it was easy to spot him as they shimmered against the light of the glowing eyes. The dragon seemed to have no regard or care for itself. It was clearly focused, and nothing could distract it from its hunt of the powerful buck. Too wide for the streets, the dragon didn't seem to think twice as it shattered windows, posts, and even full walls as it chased Johnsto relentlessly.

Cerberus had almost forgotten that the dragon had a second head, but he was quickly reminded as that second head lifted itself up above the smoke, destruction, and chaos to get a bird's-eye view of the situation. Quickly it located Cerberus, locking eyes with the tiger and flickering its tongue in a way that only a two-headed dragon would when it knew it had found two prizes in one day.

Cerberus found himself pulled into the beast's gaze. Even with the darkness and surrounding dust from the debris, he hadn't seen it this clearly since the day it had swallowed Leonidas. Trapped in a hypnotic state of shock and awe, he found himself frozen as two of the four blue eyes stared knowingly into his soul.

Back when Leonidas had been swallowed, Cerberus didn't know what to do, and this time he didn't know what to do either—but this time he knew he had to do *something*.

So, he did.

Grabbing a metal bar from the wreckage, and even though he knew one of the heads was watching him directly, Cerberus ran after the head of that beast that was pursuing his friend. He wasn't going to let what had happened to Leonidas happen to anyone else, ever again. Running across Bismarthi, along the trail of destruction, Cerberus found Johnsto cornered between three walls and the dragon's mouth. Johnsto had managed to grab one of the few lit torches as he ran, which he was now swinging back and forth to keep the monster at bay. The dragon lashed its tongue at him but stayed safely behind the torch's reach.

From above, the second head continued to watch Cerberus calmy studying his every move. Cerberus clanged the metal bar, but it was unnecessary, as he already had the dragon's attention. Having two heads made it particularly good at multitasking. As Johnsto swung his torch at the first head, the second head slowly lowered itself down to Cerberus's level. Cerberus stepped back and the beast pulled towards him. Cerberus stepped back again, and though the second head pulled, it had to stop, as the first head wasn't willing to give up on Johnsto that easily. Cerberus took another step back and the beast stretched itself between its two targets, unable to stretch any further to get one unless it gave up on the other. It was clearly unwilling to give up on either.

"Leave him alone!" Cerberus called out. "I know it's me you want!"

The Cerberus-facing head lashed its forked tongue towards him furiously. Over at front of the other head, Johnsto continued to wave his torch. "Leave Cerberus alone!" He yelled. "He's our guest and I'll do whatever I have to do to protect him!"

Light flickered in the smoke, and with a large *hiss* from each, both heads turned away from their targets quickly. Cerberus could feel heat, and suddenly his vision began to improve. The villagers had managed to re-spark the bonfire and were adding new material to build it up again quickly. The glow grew, lighting and warming Bismarthi at a fast and steady rate.

The dragon writhed in the heat, and the head facing Cerberus lurched back as the other head lunged towards Johnsto—but suddenly, it flung itself back with a pained roar. The dragon shook itself back and forth, and through the smoke, Cerberus could see that Northsie had jumped down onto its back, holding a scale with one arm, raising a metal rod with the other. Acting quickly, she plunged the metal rod directly into the back of its neck. Thick blue smoke billowed through the hole in the dragon's throat as it roared, the sound piercing the night sky. It shook, trying to fling Northsie off, but she held on tight. Looking from Cerberus to Johnsto and back to Cerberus again, she yelled, "Both of you! Run!"

But before any running could be done, the fire in the center of town swelled, and the dragon's skin started to blister. It shrieked, writhed, and slamming Northsie against a collapsing wall as it struggled to escape the nearby flames. She fell.

"No!"

Johnsto dropped his torch as he pushed under the writhing dragon's neck and made his way to her unconscious body. The dragon raised one head into the air and let out another roar, coughing as blue smoke billowed into the sky. Even its blistering skin was starting to smoke now.

Holding Northsie, Johnsto looked up at the injured head. It didn't look too good. This might be an opportunity.

"Cerberus, I think its injured. Maybe we can—"

"No, Johnsto, move!" Cerberus had seen this play before.

But Johnsto wasn't fast enough. Like a bullet, the second head whipped out of the smoke and rushed Johnsto and Northsie, smashing through the surrounding debris and swallowing them both whole.

"NO!" Cerberus ran through the mud towards the dragon, but it was already departing faster than he could wade. And while it indeed was injured, as the second head was dragged away, it managed to open its blue eyes long enough to stare deeply into Cerberus's soul. Cerberus continued to wade towards it, but it disappeared into the trees, making its way out of the light and heat of the fire and back into the shadows of darkness, down the familiar worn path towards Cathorn. And just a quickly as it had arrived, it was gone.

Cerberus fell to his knees in shock. Quickly Clora rushed to side, and together, he and the other citizens of Bismarthi watched the plume of smoke that rose above the trees trail away into the distance.

"Where's Northsie? We can't find her anywhere!" Northsie's parents were digging through the rubble frantically.

"Come on Cerberus, let's get you inside and cleaned up," Clora said as she tried to help him to his feet.

"No."

Cerberus pushed her helpful hoof off his shoulder as he stood up and kept wading through the mud.

"I have to go after them."

Finally clearing the mud and finding solid footing, Cerberus took off running towards the woods.

"Wait!" Clora called after him.

Cerberus turned back to look at her. Behind her, illuminated by the restored bonfire, he could see the other citizens of Bismarthi already working together to repair the city. They were a strong community, and he knew that they would recover.

But nobody else was going to be able to save Leonidas. Or Johnsto. Or Northsie.

Cerberus turned back towards the smoke that was quickly dissipating into the night. There was no choice to make.

"I'll bring them back! I'll bring them all back!"

Cerberus ran, disappearing into the darkness almost as quickly as the dragon had.

"I'm coming. Don't worry, I'm coming."

His voice was just a whisper now.

Soon, the town of Bismarthi was just a glowing dot in the distance behind him.

15

It took roughly twenty-three days to reach Cathorn. It had been a cold, often wet journey, yet each night Cerberus had managed to successfully light a fire. The dragon never appeared, but he could still sense it. The feeling grew stronger the closer he got to the city.

He had learned to make his own jerky and had found a couple of plants that didn't give him a stomachache when he chewed on them during the longer walking days. Not getting a stomachache was crucial for survival.

Cerberus wished he hadn't left his newly forged knife behind in Bismarthi when he fled, but the jagged piece of steel he had recently found still made for a helpful tool in his arsenal. Even though it wasn't perfect, he utilized it in nearly all his daily activities, and considered himself lucky to have found it.

The leather straps that Clora has given him were also proving extremely helpful, and even though they had never been properly turned into gloves, he had been able to use them to secure various objects, including himself, to other various objects along the journey—and when wrapped tightly around his paws, they basically did the job that gloves would've anyway.

Cerberus regretted that he and Clora had never found the time to make the new canteen for storing and boiling pure water that they had spoken of. So, as he kept moving forward, he drank water where he could. Whether it was from a passing stream or gathered up in a conical leaf after a rain; he would take as many sips as necessary and hope for the best.

During the long hike towards Cathorn, Cerberus often wondered about Johnsto. The dragon seemed to have pursued and swallowed him deliberately. Cerberus wondered why that could be. The more he thought about it, the more he realized that it didn't seem like the beast had come to Bismarthi that night for any other reason. Cerberus knew that Johnsto's grandfather had founded Bismarthi after leaving Cathorn, but other than that... well, Cerberus realized that during his stay he hadn't really learned that much about Johnsto or the history of Bismarthi at all. Ten years ago, back when Lupita the giraffe had transformed into the dragon, Cerberus had assumed that it was a result of Leonidas's experiment gone wrong, but now, with more reflection and context, it seemed that there was more to all of this than just incorrect scientific calculations.

And then there was poor Northsie, swallowed by a dragon only because tried to stick to her beliefs and what she felt was expected of her as a new adult in her community. Cerberus had been around her age when the dragon had attacked his father at the Animal Research Laboratory, and at the time he didn't have anywhere close to her level of bravery and confidence. And while he liked to think things had changed over the past ten years, deep down he still wasn't sure if he did. Johnsto wasn't even her father, yet she had confidently given everything she could to save him. Even though Cerberus's time in Bismarthi was short, truly appreciated how everyone treated each other like family, himself included. It didn't matter if he was a newcomer, or not of blood relation, they looked out for him as one of their own just the same.

Cerberus came to a place where the river forked, and following the left fork of the stream, he soon found himself approaching what could only be Cathorn. The weather on this journey had been cold already, but now it seemed to grow colder with each step. As he got closer, he could see young boars, elk, and even opossums playing in freshly fallen snow, while the adults bustled about; some working, some playing, other idly staring at the clouds. While he didn't know what he should expect, he was still surprised to find Cathorn was a full and busy city. Bismarthi was barely the size of a city block here. As Cerberus turned to take it all in, up the hills, far across the city sprawl, he spotted a massive black castle on the edge of the mountains, towering ominously.

The warm glow of lights through the window of an inn illuminated the snow in the town square. The expected warmth from within called to Cerberus, and as he approached, he noticed a statue standing nearby. Though regal in stature, it appeared to be an unfamiliar creature with a hard shell, crowned, sitting on a large throne—unlike anybody Cerberus had seen before. In one claw he held a staff, while the other appeared to be fused to the throne itself, though that could just be the fault of the artist who had sculpted it.

That must be the king, Cerberus thought as he pushed open the door to the inn.

The first room inside the inn was a pub. Cerberus took a seat at the bar, but after seventeen minutes, became annoyed that there wasn't any staff in sight, even though there were eleven other patrons spread between the barrels-turned-tables. So, he got up and looked around. To the side of the bar, he spotted a hinged door, and as he approached it, he heard voices on the other side and unintentionally began to listen in on their private conversation.

"I told you, Bernadina—" said one of them.

"—And I told you!" interrupted the other. "I've been robbed fifteen times this year, and I can't keep dealing with it! I have things to deal with at home."

"But this is an inn!" the first voice called back. "And you know my arrangement with your family. If you can't come to work—"

Cerberus had had enough eavesdropping, so he knocked on the door, and quickly scurried back to his table, hoping to blend in unnoticed. Back home he never would've intruded but living outside with only sporadic sips of water and infrequent meals consisting of mostly jerky for over twenty-three days had made him slightly more impatient. The voices on the other side of the door paused awkwardly, and suddenly the door swung open, revealing a young raccoon in an apron. Casting a furious glare, she scanned the room, hoping to spot the interrupting culprit.

"All right, who did that?"

The eleven other patrons pointed directly at Cerberus.

The racoon approached him. This must be Bernadina. She couldn't have been older than he was when his father had been taken, at the very least, she wasn't any taller. And while things in the years since had been tough for him, overhearing the conversation from behind the door, it didn't sound like things had been going well for her either, so Cerberus decided to be polite, even though it had now been over nineteen minutes. Twenty-three days of longing for a good meal was getting closer and closer to becoming twenty-four.

"I'm sorry about that," he began. "It's just that I'm very hungry."

"Oh, you're hungry?" Bernadina mocked. "What if I got hungry and walked into your house and demanded food?"

"Wait a minute, you live here? I thought you had a home."

"No, I don't live here, I was just making a—" Bernadina stopped, tilting her head at him. "Were you listening to my conversation, too?"

"I'd been waiting for a while, so I walked over, and happened to overhear—"

"All right, get out."

Cerberus couldn't believe his ears. Here he was, nearly twenty-four days away from a full meal, and he was already getting kicked out of the first restaurant he had found.

"But I'm hungry," he pleaded. "It's been twenty-th—"

"Get out of here!"

Cerberus shuffled towards the door and pushed it open. The cold wind greeted him like an old friend.

"If you're still out there after I end my shift, I'll bring you something."

Bernadina had spoken softly, but Cerberus had heard her. So, he listened, went back outside, sat by the door, and waited in the falling snow. Eventually the sun set, and Cerberus noticed a light orange glow flickering and pulsing out from the castle. Watching it dance back and forth, made him sleepy. Or maybe it was the cold air penetrating his fur. Heavy eye lids began to settle, as his head drooped into his chest. Five minutes couldn't hurt.

***

"All right, let's get out of here."

Cerberus found himself being nudged awake. Groggy, he looked up to see Bernadina, coat buttoned up and ready to go.

"To where?" Cerberus mumbled. "I thought you said you'd bring me something if I waited for your shift to end."

"I said I'd bring you something if you walked me home," Bernadina replied snappily. "From your eavesdropping, you know I've already been robbed fifteen times this year. You don't want to help keep me safe?"

Cerberus wanted to help. "But I'm so hungry."

"Fine. Here."

Bernadina tossed a leather sack to him; inside were a few biscuits. Cerberus quickly took a few bites.

"Walk me home and I'll share my roast with you."

"You have a roast?"

"You think I was just going to eat those biscuits dry?"

Cerberus had gone to culinary school; he should know better than to think anyone would eat a biscuit without an accompanying roast unless it was a last resort. Embarrassed, he stood up.

"So, it's a deal?" Bernadina asked.

"All right."

They set off from the pub, walking down the snowy streets of Cathorn together. The streets were dark and narrow, lined with doors to homes and stores that were either closed for the night, the winter, or permanently, it was hard to tell.

Bernadina trudged ahead, determined, and Cerberus hurried to keep up. She wasn't starving and knew the streets well.

If there's a fight, she might have to protect me, Cerberus thought.

Above the streets, Cerberus could still see the castle looming. It seemed like there wasn't anywhere you couldn't see it from, which must mean that whoever was up there could see everyone at any time in return.

"So, that statue near the pub," Cerberus began, between breaths.

"Of King Luridae?" Bernadina snapped back. "What about it?"

"Can you tell me about him?"

"What do you mean 'Tell me about him'?"

Apparently, Bernadina didn't have time for this. Maybe she would be more open to talking once they reached their destination.

So, in cold, snowy silence, they kept walking.

16

"We're back and didn't get robbed.
What a miracle."

Cerberus attempted his first joke in months: "It must've been because I was with you."

Bernadina ignored it as she opened her door. It stuck, so she jiggled it a bit to loosen it up. "The cold warps the wood," she muttered.

Cerberus extended a paw to help, which was ignored even more than his joke. Bernadina kept jiggling the door handle, and knowing this wasn't the first time she'd had dealt with this, Cerberus stayed quiet, waiting patiently. Soon, the wood creaked into a looser position, and a moment later the door opened. Finally, they were inside.

It had been impossible to tell from the outside, but inside, Bernadina's home was quite sizable. What was also sizable was the amount of dust covering nearly everything. Bernadina followed what seemed to be her daily evening routine, as evidenced by the lack of dust on her path and objects she interacted with, including lighting some candles and torches around the room. Above the empty fireplace, Cerberus observed a painting of several other racoons, all posed formally. This must be her family. All the dust made it clear they hadn't been around in a while.

Bernadina hung a cauldron over a large open fire in the adjacent corner of the room and began to heat up the roast. Soon, they were eating. Bernadina watched Cerberus with suspicion as he wolfed down his bowl, finishing it quickly. He looked up expectantly. Bernadina stared at him.

"You can have seconds if you want."

Cerberus did want, and soon Cerberus did have. Feeling life returning to him, he shifted closer to the fire to stay warm.

"Okay," said Bernadina. "Clearly you're not from around here, and clearly you haven't eaten in a while. I'm sure you've got a story to tell, so come on, let's hear it."

Cerberus doubted Bernadina would believe his story, so he left off the first part. He told her he had come from Bismarthi, a nearby town, where a two-headed dragon had appeared during a storm. He told her about Johnsto and Northsie and said that he had made it his responsibility to save them if it was possible, and that he had been following the dragon's trail, which had led him here.

"Here?"

"Well, not here to your house, literally. Just here to Cathorn."

Bernadina seemed to be taking this better than he expected.

"So, you say you're from Bismarthi?" she replied.

"Yeah, do you know it?"

"Founded by Alaine Dubeck?"

Cerberus didn't know Johnsto's grandfather's last name, but that sounded about right, so he nodded.

"And you don't know who King Luridae is?"

Cerberus tried to dodge the question. "Look, I'm just trying to save Johnsto and Northsie so I can bring them home. So, can you help me or not?"

Bernadina took a big bite of roast and chewed it slowly. "Well, can I trust you or not?"

"You can trust me."

"Then why are you only telling me half of the truth?"

"What?"

"You're obviously not from Bismarthi. You know that's obvious, right? So, either you tell me everything right now, honestly, or I'll put you back on the street in the snow again, and that'll be the last bite of roast you have, possibly ever."

So, Cerberus took it back to the actual beginning and told her about Leonidas, Lupita, the ARL, Ricky, Dot, the Culinary Labs, Henry B. Orenthall, and the MonFus. When he finished, Bernadina took another long breath.

"You don't believe me, do you?" Cerberus was getting frustrated. "I'm telling the truth, I really am. I know it sounds crazy."

Bernadina sighed. "Who am I to call you crazy? I've been through some crazy stuff too. Well, maybe not *that* crazy, but still."

What a relief. Cerberus was thankful.

"Since you're not from anywhere close to around here, let me fill you in as much as I can."

Bernadina leaned in closer to the fire, lowering her voice. Cerberus leaned in over his roast, as not to miss a word.

"King Luridae has been king for as long as anyone can remember. He lives in the castle up on the hill. I say 'lives,' but nobody has seen him in decades. However, his guards patrol the streets daily."

"What about the two-headed dragon?"

"Folks around have caught glimpses of it, but rarely—and I've never heard of it 'taking' anyone. Some say it lives under the castle, some say it exists to do King Luridae's bidding, but that's all just speculation."

None of this was making any sense to Cerberus. After all, he was there when Lupita transformed into the dragon, and King Luridae, or whatever-his-name-was, certainly hadn't been around when it happened. He would've remembered it.

But Cerberus wasn't even sure where he was. He had gone into the portal, sure, but it didn't seem like Ricky knew where it went either, only that it would take him to where the dragon had gone— to where Leonidas must be. And why would a king bid a dragon to take his father anyway? Or Johnsto? Or Northsie?

None of this made any sense, but one thing was for sure. If there was a chance that Leonidas was somewhere in the castle, Cerberus had to get inside to find him. "I need you to get me inside the castle," he pleaded. "If my dad may be there, you have to get me in."

Bernadina laughed, but stopped when she realized that Cerberus wasn't kidding.

She took the roast off the fire. "How am I supposed to get you into the castle?" she asked. "I just told you that nobody's seen King Luridae in decades. You don't think the castle is heavily guarded? You can't just sneak in there and poke around, hoping to find someone who was probably eaten by a dragon."

"I know he wasn't eaten."

"How do you know?"

"Ricky picked up energy readings saying that he could be here."

"Yes. But how do you *know*?" Bernadina looked through his eyes and deep into Cerberus's soul.

He sighed. "I guess I don't. But I have to try."

"But I don't," Bernadina replied quickly. "I have a pretty good life here. A home, a job at the pub. My life is happening right here, right now, and I don't need to risk it."

Cerberus had one card left to play.

"What were you arguing about at the pub?"

Bernadina frowned. "You mean when you were eavesdropping on me?"

"I told you it wasn't on purpose. But come on, I just told you everything."

Bernadina looked over at a door across the room. The lack of footprints in the dust surrounding it implied that nobody had gone through it in a while.

"You can sleep in there tonight. It's not safe to go back outside this late."

Bernadina gestured across the room towards a door as she stood up. She wasn't much taller standing than she was sitting, but it was clear that the conversation was over. "And don't think about poking through my house. The dust doesn't lie."

With that, Bernadina went into what must have been her room, shutting the door behind her. A heavy locking sound followed.

Cerberus wondered if Bernadina always locked the interior doors in her home, or if this was a special case due to not trusting her current houseguest.

The fire dwindled. Cerberus pulled out his makeshift parchment map, and using a piece of charcoal, added Cathorn and Bernadina's home to it. He looked over his journey from Bismarthi and smiled. Now that he was safe in a home, with a fire and fresh roast, the previous twenty-three days didn't feel as bad as they had before.

Cerberus packed some cool ash over the embers, and once it was safe, placed the logs from under the cauldron into the nearby fireplace, where they could smolder through the night safely. It was odd that she would light an open fire, as well as so many candles, yet leave the fireplace itself neglected. He looked up at the dimly lit family portrait. This must've been a strange place to grow up, but compared to his youth, maybe it wasn't that strange after all.

Cerberus picked up one candle, extinguished the rest, and retreated to his new room. Stepping off the dust-free path Bernadina had cleared, Cerberus realized that the thick layer of dust across the rest of her home really did highlight every single interaction.

He wiped off the door handle, and creaked open a door that clearly hadn't been touched in years. The room was spacious and practically arranged. Cerberus made his way to the bed, leaving a trail of fresh footprints behind. When he put the candle into a lantern on the bedside table, a warm glow illuminated the corner of the room, and Cerberus shook the bedding as best he could to clear off the dust that had gathered. There really was quite a cloud of it, and the way the candlelight caught the larger particles as they floated back down to the floor looked almost magical—as though the reflective sparkles would take on a life of their own, catch and spread across the home with flamboyance, burning away and restoring the true former majesty of the home underneath.

But that didn't happen. The dust simply fell out of the way of the light, settling on the floor. Cerberus climbed into the worn bed. Though he was slightly concerned about his allergies, he was cozy and safe. He extinguished the candle. As moonlight peeked through the clouded glass on the window, he realized that even from this room, he could still make out the shape of the castle, with its pale orange glow, sitting up on the mountain watching over him.

As he drifted off to sleep, Cerberus wondered about the family of racoons in the portrait above Bernadina's fireplace, and what had happened to them. Maybe Bernadina was looking for answers as well.

And with that, Cerberus fell asleep.

17

The next morning, the natural light that managed to creep through the dusty windows made the room feel much more inviting. As Cerberus awoke, he noticed clothing hanging in a left-open closet, a desk with a letter in progress, and some sports gear thrown casually into a corner—all under the now-familiar layer of undisturbed dust. Thinking back to the portrait in the other room, Cerberus assumed that this room must belong to one of the younger kids in the family.

Cerberus was happy that Bernadina had let him sleep in; his body had needed it. Now, between the roast and a good night's rest, energy was coming back, and he was beginning to feel a lot more like himself again.

Carefully retracing his dusty footprints, Cerberus made his way back to the living room. Bernadina had clearly been up for a while, and was sitting at the table, wrestling with some tools and an object of some kind. As she noticed Cerberus, she put them to the side, out of view.

"You're finally awake. Good. What did you do with the cooking fire?"

"Oh, I put it out before bed."

Cerberus's eye was drawn back to the fireplace, clean as ever, despite the ash he had dumped in it the previous night. He didn't understand why Bernadina would take the time to keep the fireplace so clean yet neglect the dust issue that had clearly overtaken the rest of her home.

In the morning light, the portrait that hung above it was much easier to study. Cerberus could make out two parents, two kids, and a baby. He figured the baby must be Bernadina and was curious as to what had happened to everyone else.

"So, was that your brother's room?"

Caught off guard, Bernadina looked up from her work. "What?"

"The room I slept in last night," Cerberus said. "Was that your brother's?"

"My sister's," Bernadina replied coldly. "And I thought I told you not to poke around."

"I wasn't poking around. I just saw some of the stuff and wondered whose room I was in."

"That sounds like poking around to me."

Bernadina got up from the table and put whatever she was working on in a drawer. After locking it carefully and placing the key in her pocket, she turned back to Cerberus.

"If you want to go see the castle today, you should eat something first."

Bernadina gestured to a loaf of bread sitting by the table. Cerberus picked it up. Unsurprisingly, it was solid as a rock. He thought about the culinary academy, where one of his first lessons had been how to store bread properly so this wouldn't happen. Even a fresh loaf would turn solid after a few hours if left sitting, and Cerberus knew that wrapping it in an airtight beeswax wrap with little to no air was the only real tried and true trick to maintain its soft and fluffy state. He considered sharing his learnings with Bernadina for her future consideration, but she cut him off before he could start.

"I have a lot to do today," Bernadina grumbled. "So, if you want me to show you how to get to the castle, you'd better hurry up and eat quickly. Better yet, take the bread for the road."

"You're going to take me to the castle?" Cerberus couldn't help but smile.

"I said I would show you how to get to the castle," Bernadina quickly corrected, as she stood by the door tapping her foot impatiently. "And I also told you to hurry up."

Quickly, Cerberus cracked off a piece of hard bread and gathered his things. Soon they were back outside, once again walking the narrow streets of Cathorn. But now, seen in daylight, and under a fresh blanket of snow, Cerberus couldn't help but think the city looked much cozier and inviting than it had the night before. Various townspeople were hard at work, shoveling their walkways clear, while their little ones played by building snow sculptures, and throwing snowballs at unsuspecting passersby. Bernadina trudged on, confidently uninterested.

"The castle is on the highest hill in this region. It's an extremely steep climb, with only one heavily secured road, so you won't be able to get that close to it," Bernadina grunted as she stomped through the snow. "But I know a smaller hill nearby that gives a decent view of the lower grounds. That's where I'm taking you."

"I thought you were going to help me break in."

"No. Like I said, I have plenty of things I need to do today, and breaking into a castle isn't one of them. I have errands to run for my job—you know, responsibilities. I can't risk everything to commit a crime with you, and honestly, you shouldn't have even told me that's what you're planning on doing. That's already implicating me in your half-baked plan, and besides, I'm already doing more than I said I would by taking you to even see the road the castle. Oh, and you can't stay with me again tonight either, you already did too much poking around my house for that to be an option."

Bernadina continued to grumble on. Cerberus finished his hard piece of bread and looked up at the approaching castle that loomed over him. Strangely, no snow sat on or surrounded the castle, even though it was at a higher elevation than the rest of Cathorn.

"Why isn't there any snow up there?" Cerberus asked.

"It must be warmer up there. Must be a climate thing. I don't know," Bernadina replied.

As they continued up, the snow dissipated, and their footsteps became more confident and less slippery. Looking back at the valley behind them, Cerberus could see just how big a city Cathorn was.

Sprawling streets seemed to go out in every direction, and the forest from which he had approached was nothing but a faded line on the horizon. There wouldn't be any point in trying to spot Bismarthi; it was an impossible distance away.

"We're nearly there," Bernadina said. "Try not to draw any attention."

As they approached the outlook, Bernadina sat down. Thoughtfully, she gestured for Cerberus to join as she set up a small picnic that he didn't realize she had prepared earlier that morning.

"Oh wow, thank you!" Cerberus said as he reached for a piece of cheese, only to get his paw slapped back.

"Don't eat anything," Bernadina scolded. "I need to bring all of this over to the inn later. It's just here for the visuals. So that if anyone sees us, they don't think we're up to anything suspicious."

So instead of satisfying his remaining hunger, Cerberus mimed eating cheese while he and Bernadina looked out castle's lower courtyard. Bernadina was right. Even though they could see into the courtyard, the rest of the castle still towered above them.

Cerberus did his best to pay close attention so that he could remember all the details, as he hoped to add them to his parchment later. He was surprised how easy it was to see into the courtyard, especially for a place that seemed to be intentionally placed in a hard-to-see area. He was also surprised at how nothing in the courtyard appeared to be unusual, despite the strange feeling he had about the area.

A few soldiers came around a corner, convening by the base of one of the castles towers. Even from a distance, Cerberus noticed that their armor appeared to be forged from a hard, shiny dark-blue material. It had a dull sheen and texture unlike any armor he had ever seen, something like the shell of a bug. It wasn't metal, it wasn't plastic, it was just something different all together. The group stopped for a minute, messing around, until another soldier, came out of the lower tower. From the way everyone else in the group snapped to attention as he approached, it was easy to assume that this one was their leader. And from the look of this leader's face, clearly the fun they were having was over. The group listened intensely as their leader delivered a brief update, departed collectively into the castle's lower tower, shutting a heavy steel door behind them.

Cerberus wondered what they were doing in there. Whatever it was it sure seemed important, but the castle only had few windows, none of which offered a peek inside to continue observing.

"Have you seen enough? I need to get on with my day."

Bernadina began packing up the picnic, and Cerberus sighed, knowing that even if he stayed in this spot longer, the odds of learning anything he hadn't already noted were low. He had assumed the castle had a courtyard and confirming that it indeed did have one didn't help develop his plan to break in any further. Still, instead of helping Bernadina pack up the uneaten picnic, Cerberus continued observing for a few moments longer. He watched as another soldier rode around the corner and into the courtyard on a buffalo-pulled cart. Once it stopped, he hopped out to open the cart's cargo bed. As if on command, the other group of soldiers emerged from the lower tower, each carrying a large, burlap sack. Each full to the brim and tied at the top, the soldiers procedurally loaded them into the cart. The group then returned to the tower to get another round of bags.

Once the cart was fully loaded, the cargo was tightly secured with rope and concealed under a large blanket. Finally, the leader climbed into the driver's seat, taking hold of the reins. The soldier who had originally delivered the cart climbed into the other seat, and an additional two from the squad jumped on the back, holding to each side of the rear. The Buffalo moved more slowly now, clearly irritated by the weight they had to carry. The carriage made its way across the grounds, and through the thick steel doors that separated the courtyard from the outside world.

Cerberus jumped up, nearly disrupting a perfectly packed picnic.

"We have to follow that cart!"

"Shh!" Bernadina reminded him, pulling him back down quickly. "You don't want to draw attention, remember? And why do you want to follow that cart, anyway? Looks like it's just full of trash."

"If it were full of trash, why would it be so heavily guarded?"

Bernadina grunted. "Regardless of your point, I still need to get back to the inn. Brogdalio already has it out for me, and I need that job."

"Okay, just help me get to that cart and then I'll go with you to the Inn and tell Brogdale that it's all my fault."

"I don't need your help. And his name's Brogdalio."

Cerberus couldn't help but pull her arm in unconscious passion, which he dropped quickly at her sight of her immediate frown.

"Please, Bernadina, I've come all this way to find my father, and this might be a clue. It could even be the only way. I can't just not investigate and learn everything I can about this place. You may not need my help, but I need yours."

Though her fist remained clenched in stress, Bernadina's face softened, and she took a slow breath.

"All right. But after I help you find that cart, we go our separate ways. I mean it!"

"Okay, okay. We can go our own ways. I promise."

"And you carry the picnic. And don't drop anything!"

Cerberus grabbed the picnic bag and quickly followed Bernadina down the hill. They lost sight of the cart as they descended, but Bernadina knew her way through the streets of Cathorn well, and following her lead, they found themselves moving from roads to rooftops, where they were easily able to watch the cart as they followed from a safe distance. As the vehicle bounced along the paved roads, Cerberus hoped that the blanket covering the cargo would flap up enough for him to peek under and see what was in the bags they were transporting. But the blanket was wrapped tightly, and peeking would have to wait.

"Where do you think this thing is going, anyway?"

The cart exited the city roads and turned down a path that wound up towards the mountains.

"If I knew, I would be back at the inn by now. Just follow it."

Climbing down from the rooftops to even footing, they let the cart move further ahead, intentionally creating more distance as they continued to follow the path up the barren stone mountainside.

Nearing a plateau, Cerberus and Bernadina watched the cart disappear behind a protruding stone wall.

"I don't know how we can follow that road without them seeing us."

Bernadina scanned the area, noticing a smaller path to the side.

"That looks like a path as well. The cart is too big to pass through it, but we should be able to get through just fine. If we go this way, then they won't be able to see us. Come on."

Cerberus didn't have to be told twice. He and Bernadina helped each other along the narrow, path carefully. Finally, they emerged behind a different section of the stone wall. From this new vantage point, they could peek over the wall, where they found that the cart had finally stopped next to a large boulder that sat in the center of the stony plateau.

The leader hopped off first, followed by the other soldiers. Detaching a steel paddle with a long handle from the cart, they approached the boulder, and using the paddle as a lever, dislodged it from its position. As they cautiously rolled the boulder to the side, a dark blue light bubbled out from underneath it, revealing that it had been blocking—or plugging—a hole of some kind.

"I don't believe it," Cerberus gasped. "That looks like a portal…"

"Like the one you took to get here?" said Bernadina. "What would something like that be doing all the way up here?"

As the boulder was rolled safely away, the soldiers went to work unloading the cart's precious cargo. One by one, they each opened the burlap sacks, carefully dumping the contents into the hole. From their vantage point up on the rocky wall, Cerberus did his best to watch without being spotted. Whatever was in the bags looked like warped plastic mesh, with flashes of blue and purple, almost like large pieces of glitter. As it was poured into the hole, it flickered with flashes of light and puffs of brightly colored smoke.

Bernadina pulled Cerberus's arm to refocus his attention.

"Look."

She nodded over at the leader, who was opening the final sack. Finishing their work, the others gathered around him, excitedly. The leader reached in and pulled out a of couple pawfuls of the stuff, which he tossed to the others. With each catch, the soldiers smiled wickedly, clearly this wasn't the first time they had kept a little for themselves.

"Job well done," the leader said.

The soldiers complimented him right back, and one by one they rubbed the glittery material over their armor, helping each other spread it over all the hard-to-reach areas. The cracks between the chitin plating began to glow with a bright neon hue as the materials merged. Each soldier took a deep breath with a shudder, as they shook in their armor, settling once again.

"Alright now, let's hurry back to the castle."

The leader and his squadron packed up the empty sacks and assumed their previous positions on the cart once again. Slowly the cart started to move.

"What do you think they were doing?" Cerberus whispered.

"We need to go before they notice us." Bernadina stressed.

"No! We've got to investigate that hole once they leave."

Cerberus resisted, but as he pulled from Bernadina's grip on his shoulder, the picnic slipped from her arms, crashing on the ground in a sound that could only be described as *'announcing their hidden presence loudly and with confidence'*.

"I think someone is watching us," a soldier muttered, gesturing to bring the cart to a slow stop.

"Hey!"

Bernadina and Cerberus froze in their places.

"Well, what are you waiting for?" the leader grunted with frustration.

"Don't worry, Maximo. I'll get them," a soldier said.

Despite what looked like heavy armor, the soldier had the ability of an acrobat, and very quickly scaled the stone wall and located where Cerberus and Bernadina were still frozen in place.

"Strange place for a picnic, isn't this?" The soldier smiled, gabbing each of them on the shoulder with a firm grip. He quickly patted them down.

"I think I'll hold on to these," he said with a grin as he took not only the picnic, but Cerberus's map and sharp piece of metal as well.

"Don't worry," he called down to the others. "I took their stuff."

The drop from their vantage point down to the plateau didn't look very far, but as Cerberus and Bernadina hit the ground, thrown by the soldier from above, they were happy it wasn't any further.

Looking up, they were greeted by the glaring cold face of at the leader of the squadron, who was apparently named Maximo.

"So, let's get to the point. Who are you, why are you here, and what did you see?" he asked coldly.

As unfamiliar as he was with this place, even Cerberus knew these were questions he shouldn't answer.

"I say we just throw them in the hole," another soldier called. The rest of the group cheered along, in full support of seeing what would happen if they did.

"Nothing goes in the hole besides the cargo," Maximo growled firmly as he turned back to quiet his soldiers.

From where he lay, Cerberus could see a small, flat, sharp metal object slightly protruding from the edge of the glowing hole. Uncertain, yet compelled, Cerberus took advantage of the distracted soldiers to quickly grab it, tucking it into a flap of his clothing, unnoticed.

"Even if we're not throwing you in the hole, that doesn't mean you're safe."

Maximo laughed with menace as he refocused his attention on Cerberus and Bernadina.

"There's no reason I can't execute you both right here and now."

Maximo gripped the hilt of his sword tightly.

"So once again, what are you doing here and who are you?"

Bernadina briefly glanced at Cerberus with an apologetic look that could only be described as *preparing to cast him aside in favor of her own self-preservation'.*

"I'll be honest, he made me come here," Bernadina stammered. "I didn't want to. I knew it was a bad idea. I barely even know him. I just need to get to work. I'm already late enough as is, and I can't get fired now, I—"

Maximo waved a gloved paw in her face, as he turned his gaze to look directly into Cerberus's eyes.

"So, you're the troublemaker, then. You don't look familiar, where are you from?"

"I need to speak with King Luridae," Cerberus replied. "It's urgent."

"Oh, really?" Maximo raised an eyebrow. "Nobody speaks with the king."

"I need to warn him. There's a dragon that took my father. I followed it here to Cathorn, and I believe it's living under your castle, and it's extremely dangerous. I need to warn the king before it's too late."

Maximo's eyes gleamed. "A dragon took your father and is living under our castle? Well, that *is* concerning."

"So, we can go?" Bernadina asked hurriedly.

"No, no. We couldn't possibly just let you go. This sounds very urgent," Maximo sounded earnest. "We'll take you both back to see King Luridae, as this young tiger has requested."

Cerberus's eyes lit up. "You will? Oh, thank you!"

"Of course. But forgive me, the only way into the castle is a secret, and blindfolds just won't do."

With that Maximo raised his heavily armored paw up over Cerberus's head and brought it down quickly.

With a crack, everything went dark.

18

Cerberus awoke to a familiar tingle down his spine and a throbbing headache. As he rubbed the sore spot on the back of his head, the room around him came into focus.

There wasn't much light, but Cerberus didn't need much to see that he was in a dungeon. Beyond the bars of his cell, a torch against the wall cast a warm glow, and a single ray of bluish moonlight fell from a barred window at the top of the dungeon ceiling. The height of the window strongly discouraged any considerations regarding escape attempts, and Cerberus reasoned that it was very possible that he was being held underground. Through the faint light Cerberus could see something shift on other side of the cell, and he redirected his focus towards it.

"Bernadina? Is that you?"

"I'm not talking to you anymore."

Though the dim light made it hard to confirm, Cerberus was pretty sure that a frustrated Bernadina was sitting on the other side of the cell.

"What did I do?"

Bernadina did not feel the need to answer this question.

"Did they knock you out too? Do you know where we are?"

Cerberus reached his paw through the bars to jiggle the door handle from the other side. It didn't work, but at least he was trying.

Bernadina, however, didn't seem interested in moving a muscle.

"Would you mind helping me?" Cerberus called over, unable to mask the sound of annoyance in his voice. "We should really try to get out of here. I can't rescue my father if I'm—"

Bernadina took a deep breath, cutting Cerberus off, as she continued to ignore him.

"Bernadina please, I need your—"

That was the last straw.

"You need, you need, you need! It's all about you, isn't it?" Bernadina spat.

"No, it's not all about *me*. It's about my father. I'm trying to rescue my father. You know that," Cerberus replied in defense.

"Yesterday I had a job. Yesterday I had a home. Everything was fine, and then—"

"Everything wasn't fine!" Cerberus interrupted. "You were arguing with your boss about robberies, and living in, living in, I don't even know how to describe the state of your dusty house, but it sure wasn't *fine*!"

"And then *you* showed up and you needed food, and I gave you food," Bernadina pushed on. "Then you needed a place to stay, and I gave you a place to stay. Then you wanted to get to the castle, and against my better judgment, I took you there. And now look at us. All this for what? To rescue your father? Your father, the scientist, who was eaten by a dragon and taken through a portal that you followed that brought you to my door? You were nearly dead when you found me! How do I know you're not making all of this up?"

"But *you* knew about the dragon!" Cerberus pleaded. "You saw the hole that the guards were dumping those sacks into on top of the mountain. You know something strange is happening here!"

"And so, what if there is? I just gave up everything to help you! Maybe I shouldn't have. Sure, everything wasn't 'fine,' but at least I was surviving. At least I didn't have King Luridae's attention. They're going to ransack my home now. If what you claim is true, then you don't know what it's like living here. If we survive this, and I doubt we will, I'll be left with nothing."

Bernadina swiftly wiped away a tear that had somehow found its way from her eye to her cheek.

"I don't know why I ever agreed to help you."

Cerberus took this all in quietly. He thought about Bernadina and her job at the inn. It was strange to see such a young raccoon working at a place like that. He thought about her large home, and how strangely unoccupied and dusty it was. He thought about the portrait of Bernadina's family that he had seen hanging above the fireplace and wondered what had happened. Where were all those other raccoons? Suddenly it all came together.

"Because you lost somebody, too," he said quietly. "But you still have hope that they can be found again, just like I do."

Bernadina's eyes broke away from Cerberus's gaze, but before she could respond a low rumble echoed up through the walls, seemingly from depths far below the dungeon. Cerberus winced in pain as his spine tingled. It had never hurt like that before.

Bernadina wiped her eyes quickly. "What was that?"

Cerberus rubbed his back to soothe the pain, at least the areas his paws could reach. "The two-headed dragon," he replied. "It must be somewhere nearby."

As he rubbed his back, Cerberus realized he could feel something strange in his pocket. The flat piece of metal he had pulled from the hole. Commotion sounded from the hallway, and unseen keys jingled against the door to the dungeon from the other side. Figuring it wasn't a good idea to get caught with a potential weapon, especially when all of his belongings had already been confiscated earlier. Cerberus quickly stashed the metal against the back of the cell.

The dungeon lock finally clicked, and the heavy door slowly swung open, allowing two guards to enter.

"Ah, good, you're both up," one said.

"The king is ready to see you," said the other.

"Try not to say anything stupid," Bernadina mumbled.

There were a lot of stairs to climb, and walking up them in shackles wasn't easy. As Cerberus climbed, he felt the temperature in the air around him rising dramatically. The color of the guards' armor seemed to shift from dark grey to blue-black in sync with the growing heat, and with each step, Bernadina's breath shortened.

Cerberus noticed the art displayed throughout the castle halls—portraits, paintings, and sculpture—yet none of it looked familiar, and some of it looked especially out of place. Sure, there were the to-be-expected portraits of successful conquests and presumably powerful families, but there were also paintings that seemed much older, of strange creatures pushed far into abstraction. In one image, two furless paws were held up to the sides of a colorful, contorted face making a horrifying expression, and another showed a tan being with long brown hair on its head smirking at the foreground of a vague landscape. Cerberus understood that art wasn't always intended to be realistic, but these pieces took surreal to a whole different level, almost as if it had been acquired from another universe entirely.

Two ominous large doors stood shut at the end of the hall, and the guards stopped Cerberus and Bernadina as they approached.

"Behind these doors awaits the throne room, one said.

"If you value your life, you will be respectful," the other cautioned.

Slowly, the guards opened the heavy doors, revealing the long and dark throne room on the other side, with the only cast light coming from the hallway in which the group currently stood. Cerberus squinted, trying to see if anyone was seated in the throne that presumably sat on the other side, but unfortunately that side of the room was completely concealed in heavy shadow.

"Well, what are you waiting for?"

The guard closest to Cerberus shoved his armored elbow into the tigers back, forcing him to stumble forward and into the room. Catching his balance, and taking slow, careful steps, Cerberus and Bernadina found themselves inside. As if by automation, the large doors behind them swung shut of their own accord, and leaving the tiger and racoon separated from the guards and completely shrouded in the hot darkness.

"What do we do?" Cerberus's voice trembled.

"Shh. Keep walking."

Together, they each took another cautious step forward. In strange sync to their steps the room itself rumbled, and a deep cracking sound sputtered, as if someone were trying to use a pillow to cover the sound of a nearby splitting rock.

"What's that?"

Cerberus couldn't even see Bernadina, who was still presumably right next to him, so being asked what something further away was seemed close to impossible, but slowly, his vision began to improve as a red light swelled into focus on each side of the hall, casting its glow across the floor.

"Where's that light coming from?"

"I think it's coming from up there."

Sure enough, high on the opposing walls on both the left and right of the room, small openings in the stone glowed red, as narrow stream of bright orange fluid began to pour. The room felt even hotter as the two streams flowed into cut grooves in their respective wall, each moving towards the distant end of the throne room. The little light cast was far overpowered by the accompanying heat.

Cerberus and Bernadina continued to move forward, and a few steps later, it happened again. Out of two more parallel openings against each side of the room, more of the orange liquid began to pour.

"Don't touch it, it's hot," Cerberus warned.

"Yeah, I figured as much."

"This liquid must be why it's so hot up here."

"You think?"

Though Cerberus could now see Bernadina more clearly, the end of the throne room was still concealed in shadow. Still, with every few steps, more valves would open, allowing more fluid to flow down the walls towards the end of the room. As streams combined, a little bit of the fluid splashed to the floor, turning dark and solid as it cooled quickly once separated from the source.

With each new flow, the light grew brighter, and the other side of the throne room came into view. Cerberus and Bernadina wiped sweat off their brows, the temperature was close to unbearable.

"I think we should stop here," Cerberus gestured.

"You don't need to tell me twice."

Just ahead of them the molten fluid paths pulsed and twisted, flowing consciously together into one unified stream that vanished under a wide stone platform that supported a large throne made from both stone and iron, upon which sat the hulking form of the king.

"Something's off about this." Cerberus whispered.

"Shh!" Bernadina grimaced.

The King Luridae who sat before them looked exactly like the statue Cerberus had seen near the inn in Cathorn, down to the claws and the dark chitin shell plating. And just like the statue, this king Luridae also held perfectly still. Confused, Cerberus looked around the room.

"Bernadina, I don't know what all that red hot liquid was about, but I think this is just a statue. Come on let's just go back and—"

As Cerberus stepped back from the statue, the floor rumbled underneath him.

"So, you must be Cerberus."

The deep voice spoke slowly. Though it was unclear where it had originated from, it was impossible to miss. Bernadina immediately dropped into a low kneeling bow.

"Your father has told me all about you, but I never expected to meet you for myself."

The voice bounced along the room, echoing over itself. Cerberus looked around to find the source. It felt as though there could be many.

"Where are you?" A fearful Cerberus called out as politely as possible.

"I'm right in front of you."

The many echoes of King Luridae's voice reverberated and

consolidated, becoming one.

Crack.

The sound made Cerberus jump. Even Bernadina took a step back, falling over her shackles as the claws on the statue in front of them twisted suddenly and unnaturally. Through the newly formed cracks a bright orange light emanated, pulsing, reminiscent of the fluid that had previously worked its way through the room.

Crack. Crack. Crack.

The statue shifted its weight, and rose, adjusting its neck and stretching, bleeding more orange light through its material with each motion. As the cracks glowed and layers of shaken dust fell to the floor, the statue of King Luridae's figure awoke. With surreal motion, the head leaned forward towards them. As it stretched its neck, molten fluid dripped across the floor of the throne room.

Cerberus found himself back next to Bernadina, as the living arachnid-bodied statue of King Luridae adjusted again, lowering itself to perfectly match his eye level. Cerberus could feel his whiskers beginning to singe from the emanating heat. Finally, the king stopped moving. The pulsing glow seemed to cool slightly. Cerberus exhaled a quick breath of relief into the hot air.

Crack.

King Luridae's eyes snapped opened, bright orange, with molten white centers, framed by layers of dark blue-black exoskeleton plating. The plating below the eyes cracked and adjusted, melting, freezing, and cracking again, as a new space opened on the face—a mouth, from which came a deep but unmistakably clearly voice.

"Can't you see me, child?"

19

Back when Cerberus was a kidden in Leonidas's workshop, he had come across a series of drawings of eight-legged creatures. Curious to learn more, he had asked his father about them, and Leonidas was happy to share. These ancient creatures were known historically as *arachnids*, and there were several types of them, the most common two being the *spider* and the *scorpion*. While both had a hard exterior, an *exoskeleton*, as Leonidas had called it, the spider was known for having a painful bite, fuzzy hair, and more eyes than the usual two pair. The scorpion on the other hand, had a normal number of eyes, but a sharp, curved, tail full of a venom, pinching claws, and a much longer body. Looking at King Luridae now, Cerberus was most reminded of a scorpion, except that scorpions were supposed to be small creatures, and Leonidas had certainly never mentioned them radiating any substantial amount of heat or molten fluid. So, while the king did have claws, and a hard exoskeleton, for the moment it felt most accurate to consider him to simply be some sort of hard-shelled arachnid-type being filled with living magma. Especially since Cerberus had yet to confirm if he had a sharp, curved, tail full of venom or not.

The king continued to examine Cerberus closely. Though nervous, Cerberus wondered what the king was making of him. He was clearly a tiger, and there really wasn't much more to it than that.

"You said my father told you all about me? How do you know my father?"

The king stared for a moment more. Then seemingly satisfied

with his assessment, pulled back, to lean comfortably in his throne, his outer layer cracking and revealing his dripping, molten interior with every motion.

"As you were brought to me, I'll ask my questions first."

The king spoke in a relaxed growl.

"But I have heard about you, Cerberus, and I must admit I'm very curious. I can only imagine what you're doing here."

"I'm here to find my father, Leonidas. He was taken by a two-headed dragon that I believe could be living under your castle. You may all be in very real danger!" Cerberus spoke confidently. It was now or never.

The king shifted his head towards Bernadina.

"You led him to me?"

Bernadina hung her head low.

"Not intentionally. I—"

"So, you're a traitor."

Bernadina's head shot up.

"What, no! I don't even know him. I— he made—"

"Traitors rot in dungeons."

King Luridae lifted a claw, and with a click, Maximo emerged from the dark shadows behind them.

"Hey! I—" Bernadina yelped.

"Shhhh," King Luridae replied calmly. "It can always get worse."

Bernadina struggled to hold her tongue as Maximo grabbed her shackles and dragged her from the room. Soon the sound of chains scraping against the hard basalt floor faded away.

King Luridae turned back to Cerberus.

"Don't worry. You're not a traitor. You're just a scared little tiger, looking for his father. Did I hear that right?"

"Yes."

"So, how did you get here?"

Cerberus looked back towards where Bernadina had vanished to. One wrong word and he knew his quest would end here and now.

"Come on, little tiger," the king beckoned with a threatening smile. "You don't have to keep secrets from me. I know you're not from around here."

Cerberus lifted his head, struggling to avoid making eye contact.

"In fact," the king continued, "I know a lot more about you than you think."

"Do you know where my father is?"

"Of course, I do."

"Aren't you worried about the dragon? It's huge and dangerous, it could attack any moment!"

"Don't worry child, everything will be all right, I assure you. Now, hold up your arms."

Cerberus cautiously tilted his head back as he lifted his bound wrists into the air. King Luridae reached out towards them with a long, burning hot claw.

"Please, please. I haven't done anything to betray you. I—"

Clink.

Cerberus opened one eye to see his shackles fall to the ground, red hot from where the king had clamped them. They had been very tight, and almost at once, Cerberus could feel the blood flow returning to his paws.

King Luridae clicked his claw again and another soldier emerged from the shadows where Maximo had stood. Had they been watching them this whole time?

"Take our guest to his room. Be sure that he is ready for dinner this evening."

The guard's grip on Cerberus's shoulder was so firm, it was impossible to tell if it was a friendly gesture or a threat. As Cerberus turned away to follow his escort, King Luridae spoke once more.

"Don't let first impressions get the best of you. You'll see that I'm not so bad."

Cerberus glanced back just quickly enough to catch the orange glow vanishing, leaving the throne room once again shrouded in the darkness that had filled it when they had first entered. The temperature was much cooler now, and Cerberus finally felt safe enough to breath calmly once again.

***

Led down a series of dark, confusing hallways, Cerberus found himself in his new room. Strangely enough, this room looked as though it had been prepared specifically for him. Clothes that appeared to be his size hung on a rack, and a small portrait of him as a kidden sat framed on the bedside.

But that wasn't all.

Photos of bears, ducklings, platypuses, and even giraffes adorned the walls. All the creatures that Cerberus and Ricky used to dream about as kiddens. There was no way it was a coincidence. Charts and graphs were stacked on a corner desk, and thumbing through them quickly, Cerberus noticed a few schematics of the portal that Leonidas had built back at the ARL long ago.

"How did all of this stuff get here?" Cerberus wondered aloud.

"I don't know," sneered the guard, who was still standing in the doorway. "I'm not the decorator."

With that, he closed the door, and Cerberus was left in the room alone.

It was chilly, so he grabbed a blanket that was hanging on the back of a chair and wrapped it around his shoulders while he took a moment to think. He thought about Bernadina and wondered where Maximo had taken her. Back to the dungeon, most likely. Her involvement in all of this was his fault, and he'd have to do his best to get her out of there as soon as he could.

Cerberus looked out of a narrow window over the city. It was true; you could really see every street in Cathorn from up here. The sun was still high, so Cerberus figured that it would be a couple of hours before he was called to dinner. Would that be enough time to rescue Bernadina and figure out where his father was? Either way, he had to try.

Cerberus explored the room, examining everything in close detail. He ran his paws over each surface, cautiously feeling for any buttons that could lead to trap doors or reveal other hidden secrets.

When no buttons were found, he began lifting all the objects in the room, seeing if anything functioned as a switch or lever of some kind. Candlesticks, books, cups, everything in sight. He even tried turning the mirror that sat at the washing tub towards the sun, reflecting the light across the room to see if anything special would be revealed by the refraction. It was a long shot, but worth it.

A knock sounded against the door, and Cerberus dropped the mirror. Hitting the stone floor, it shattered instantly. Back home, that usually meant bad luck was coming. Then again, he had already been subjected to so much bad luck that maybe here this meant the opposite.

The knock sounded again, a little louder this time, and Cerberus went to open the door. Standing quietly in front of him, eyes pointed towards the ground, stood a young servant, holding a jug of tea along with a tray of jerky. Though her beautiful colored robes had been replaced with simple cloth, Cerberus still recognized her at once.

"Northsie?"

"I have your afternoon tea and jerky ready," Northsie said quietly, as she entered the room modestly.

"I can't believe you're here!" Cerberus whispered to her excitedly. "I'm going to get us out of here. You, Johnsto, my dad, Bernadina— you haven't met her yet, but you're both the same age. I—"

Carefully, Northsie placed the tray down at the bedside and poured Cerberus a large mug of hot tea. As she turned back towards the door, her eyes noticed the shattered glass by the window.

"It's good to see you, Cerberus. I'll send somebody to clean that glass up and will be back in a few hours to fetch you for dinner."

And with that, Northsie was gone, closing the door behind her.

Dumbfounded, Cerberus sat down on the bed. This hardly seemed like the headstrong, confident, Northsie he had met back in

Bismarthi. What had happened to her? Clearly, she had survived being swallowed by the two-headed dragon, which must mean that Johnsto and his father had as well. Ricky's theory was being proven to be accurate. This revelation was starting to shed light on how the king would have met Leonidas, but if Leonidas had been here, where was he now? Could Johnsto possibly be with him?

Cerberus was full of questions, but Northsie had said she was sending someone to clean up the broken glass, so he would have to wait until they were finished before he could resume his escape attempt. Otherwise, he risked being caught.

As Cerberus waited, he examined the books on the nearby shelf and found one about Cathorn's history. He began to flip through, scanning for anything that could possibly be considered relevant. Even if nobody here was going to tell him the information he wanted to know, this book might have something worth learning as books often did.

According to the book, Cathorn was an old kingdom, one of the oldest. In fact, it predated written history, and seemingly time itself. Cathorn was ruled by King Luridae Igneous and was described as a spark of life grown from the ashes; connected to the time before time began, a time before the *First Moments*.

Another knock at the door startled Cerberus, and he realized that he had been reading for a while. The sun was now much lower, it must almost be time for dinner. He put the book next to his bedside so he could revisit it later. Opening the door, he again found Northsie standing on the other side.

"You haven't changed for dinner," she said. "Did the clothes not fit?"

Cerberus didn't realize that he had been expected to change for dinner, so he went over to the closet to see what was on the rack. Northsie peered into the room behind him.

"Nobody came to clean up the glass?" she asked, less than enthusiastically. "I'm so sorry. I'll make sure someone comes by while you're at dinner."

Cerberus stepped behind a privacy screen, pulled on a fresh outfit, and unsurprisingly, it was a perfect fit. It had been a while since Cerberus had worn something clean, and as strange as the situation was, it felt great to wear a set of fresh, new clothes.

"Are you ready?" Northsie asked.

Cerberus hopped over to the door as he finished pulling on some boots. Together, they stepped out into the hallway.

"I'm working on a plan to get us out of here," Cerberus whispered quietly as they walked.

"I don't need to 'get out of here,'" Northsie said, keeping her eyes forward. "I've joined this community, and I'm happy to support and care for it through the completion of my daily chores."

The rest of the walk back to the throne room was a quiet one.

A long stone table had been set up down the center of the throne room. Though the room was still dark, hot, and lit only by flowing magma, the sight of fruit, meat, and vegetables on the table made for a much more welcoming experience. At the head of the table, King Luridae's solid form sat, creaks and cracks still glowing orange with every motion. At his right sat Maximo, sternly, chitinous armor glowing with hints of blue.

Nobody spoke as Northsie walked Cerberus along the length of the table, sitting him at the king's left, across from Maximo, in the only remaining seat. She then proceeded to fill three glasses of water. Cerberus assumed that King Luridae's glass was only a pleasantry; given his molten interior, it didn't seem like he was going to drink it.

Maximo, however, threw his head back and drank his water quickly. It was very hot in the room, so Cerberus didn't blame him. Northsie returned with a refill, and then exited the room.

"What have you done to her?" Cerberus turned towards King Luridae.

"You speak out of line to your king," Maximo growled from across the table.

"He's not my king."

Maximo pushed his chair back furiously, as King Luridae raised a claw.

"Patience. Maximo. This kidden is new here. He'll soon learn."

Cerberus noticed that King Luridae had said *kidden*, not *cubbin*. Maybe he had learned the word from Leonidas.

King Luridae turned to face Cerberus. "You may not understand it, but indeed, I am your king. I always have been and always will be."

"All hail King Luridae!" Maximo snapped to attention without hesitation.

"And as for her," King Luridae continued. "She's an adult and can make her own choices. I invited her to be a member of our community, and she chose to become one."

"What were her other options?" Cerberus muttered.

"She's not the one I wanted anyway, just a casualty, if that gives you any peace of mind. We were only after the buck you call Johnsto. But she interfered, just as you did. You seem to like interfering. That's what I like about your family."

"My family?"

"Your family. Your father," King Luridae smiled.

"You said you know where he is. Are you ever going to tell me?"

Maximo's fist hit the table. "You will respect your king!"

"Maximo!" King Luridae's eyes glowed towards Maximo, who grunted and picked up a tea leaf from the table. He began to chew it begrudgingly, eyes locked on Cerberus.

The king turned back to the tiger. "And your little friend? Are you going to tell me how you wound up with that rat?"

Cerberus scowled. "She's a racoon. I asked her to help me find you. She's helping me find my family, and I'm helping her find hers."

Maximo laughed, choking on his tea leaf. Making a disgusting sound, he coughed, spit it onto the floor next to his seat and wiped his mouth with his armored sleeve.

Cerberus glared at him. "What's so funny?"

"Her family?" Maximo laughed again. "We threw them into the incinerator years ago!"

"What?!" Cerberus tried to leap from his chair, but he realized the warm stone had somehow bent itself around him, restraining him to his seat.

"And you just brought the only one who got away back to us." Maximo smiled as he took a long sip from his water.

"How could you *do* that?"

"Cerberus, you seem to have a way of befriending my enemies," King Luridae spoke softly. "The rat. The buck. Everyone who wants to take from me seems to want to give to you. Would you mind helping me understand why?"

"What could Bernadina have done to you?"

"They wanted to overthrow my rule. They held meetings in secret, they evaded my guards, they cheated on their taxes. They're traitors. They wanted to kill me. Their king. Your king. They just couldn't understand that there would be nothing if not for me."

"All hail King Luridae!" Maximo chanted.

"That's very cruel for a king," Cerberus said.

Maximo leaned forward aggressively. His chair seemed to be restraining him as well.

"If you live to be as old as I am, you'll understand," King Luridae said. "And I hope you live until you do. I have important plans for you, young Cerberus. Now eat, and then I have something to show you."

"I don't know if I'm hungry now."

"I wouldn't refuse my hospitality," the king said. Who knows if you'll get this chance again?"

The stone restraint relaxed its grip, freeing Cerberus. Reluctantly, he leaned forward, took a few bites from his plate, and swallowed slowly. King Luridae smiled.

"There we go. I know this is new to you, but it will all make sense soon."

From out in the hallway, a quiet knock echoed against the steel doors.

"And speaking of."

The steel doors creaked open, and Cerberus turned to see Northsie again, but this time she was with someone else.

He had aged gracefully, much less than Cerberus would've expected given how long it had been. Besides a few grey whiskers and deepened crinkles in his face, he looked almost the same as he did the day Cerberus had last seen him.

"Dad?"

"Cerberus? Is that really you? I've missed you so much little one."

The floor sizzled with steam as tears fell from Cerberus's eyes as he rushed towards his father's side. Leonidas caught him in a strong hug.

"I never thought I'd see you here. You look older; how long has it been for you?"

"Ten years."

"Interesting," Leonidas said. "And how's your mother?"

"She's doing well, but I have to tell you, she remarried," Cerberus said. He wasn't sure what the right response was for this type of situation, so he added, "He's a pretty boring guy, though."

"She remarried?"

Leonidas had a twinge of hurt in his voice as he looked off into the distance with watery eyes. "I suppose I can't blame her. It has been a very long time."

"We missed you so much, Dad."

"I've missed you too."

Tears rolled down Leonidas's crinkled cheeks.

"So much."

The sound of Maximo's empty water glass hitting the table reminded everyone that Leonidas and Cerberus weren't the only two in the room. Northsie hurried back over to refill it.

"Why don't you join us at the table?" King Luridae beckoned.

A fourth stone seat had appeared at the table next to Cerberus's own. The father and son pair returned to the table as Northsie hurried to place a fourth setting and additional glass of water.

King Luridae raised his glass of water in his claw to the group. It bubbled as it quickly boiled at his touch.

"Leonidas, we could not be more overjoyed that your son has decided to join us here in Cathorn. We've already set him up with a fine room, provided your research for his study, and tomorrow, he'll join you in your lab to help complete the A.R.C.H. Project."

"Wait, no—" Cerberus turned to the king. "I'm not here to work. I'm here to bring him back home."

"Why would you want to take him home when his work here is so much more valuable?" the king replied. "You've been looking for him, and now you've found him. What else do you need? Your mother is remarried, and together they have their child, Stephenson. Their lives are complete. What difference does it make where you are as long as you and your father have each other? This is all you've ever wanted."

"Having two brilliant scientists in the lab will be better than one," Maximo added.

"Three," the king said.

"You know how I feel about that old relic," Maximo huffed.

"You would be nothing if not for Sal," King Luridae scowled.

Cerberus could feel the temperature in the room rise with the king's anger. Maximo returned to sipping his glass of water.

"So, there we have it," King Luridae cracked a smile. "Tomorrow the father and son tigers will join each other in the lab for a meeting of the minds."

This had never been Cerberus's plan. Yes, he was there to reunite with and rescue his father, but he was also the only one who could help Bernadina. Furthermore, he had no idea what had happened to Johnsto and needed to find out. It was also incredibly unsettling that the king knew so much about his mother, Henry B. Orenthall, and Stephenson. With so much uncertainty, Cerberus knew that the risk of what he was about to say was incredibly high. Still, he said it anyway.

"And what if I refuse?"

King Luridae's smile stayed on his molten, stone face. "I advise you to make the right decision," the king replied. "And if you do, we won't throw your friend, the rat, into the incinerator."

Leonidas wrapped his arm around Cerberus's shoulder. "I'll take him down to the lab and give him the tour."

"Very good, Leonidas," King Luridae said. "We really could use more folks like you around here."

"Shall I accompany them?" Maximo stood up with the rest, as King Luridae remained in place.

"No, Maximo," King Luridae said. "You have important business of your own to attend to."

The king turned back to the young tiger.

"Welcome to your new home, Cerberus. We are indeed grateful to have you."

20

Leaving the throne room, Cerberus followed Leonidas down a series of hallways, eventually arriving at a steel plate elevator with two heavy cables on either side.

"So how are we going to get out of here?" Cerberus asked.

"What do you mean? You're here to help me and Sal," Leonidas replied.

"What? I—"

Leonidas held his paw up to his mouth subtly, yet clearly signaling silence.

"I just can't believe you're here," Leonidas said. "I never thought I'd see you again."

They both stepped on to the elevator, and Leonidas adjusted a lever, shifting weights above them. The plate began to lower down a dark shaft, and as the tigers descended, Cerberus could feel the temperature around him beginning to cool. A light shudder flickered up his spine.

"I can't believe it's been ten years," Cerberus said.

"Ten years? For me, it's been twenty-five."

Finally, the elevator ride ended with a light bump as it settled on the ground. It was noticeably colder, so Leonidas took a jacket off a hook by the elevator door and tossed it to Cerberus, before putting on his own.

"It's colder down here," Leonidas said, "because the king keeps all the heat up there with him."

Cerberus followed his father down a short hallway which was capped by a heavy door. Producing a key from his pocket, Leonidas unlocked it. They entered, and Leonidas locked the door behind him.

"We have to be careful what we say and where we say it Cerberus," Leonidas said. "The king is always listening."

"What do you mean?"

"If you're in the castle, he can almost always hear you. His molten core flows through the hollow walls. He's everywhere up there."

"He's doesn't come down here?"

"Not that I'm aware. He won't come down here because of—"

"The dragon," Cerberus cut Leonidas off. "I could feel it in my spine as we came down in the elevator. The dragon must live down here, and the king doesn't like to get close to it because the dragon hates the heat."

"Very good little one," Leonidas nodded. "But the dragon lives much lower. We're somewhere in the middle. Between the two. Come and see the lab."

The tigers continued, entering a lab that seemed far too modern for everything else Cerberus had seen in Cathorn so far. Computers and machines buzzed and whirred, and across the room, a portal structure stood. It reminded Cerberus so much of the old ARL that he stumbled.

"It's all right. Go on in."

"What did you mean when you said that for you it's been twenty-five years?" Cerberus asked.

"It's hard to explain," Leonidas said.

"It's not that hard," another voice called out.

Cerberus jumped. Someone else was in the room with them. He looked around but saw nobody.

"Okay, Sal," said Leonidas. "Do you want to explain?"

"Sure," Sal's disembodied voice said. "It's simple."

Leonidas walked over to a table covered in equipment in the middle of the room. A steel jar with a glass dome sat at the end. Leonidas turned it around, and Cerberus jumped again.

Inside the glass dome sat a disembodied head. However, unlike most heads in jars, this one was very much alive. It looked unlike anything Cerberus had ever seen before. The nose was small and pointed, and where fur should be, there was bare pinkish skin. Maybe there was a little peach fuzz on it, but this was the least-furry head Cerberus had ever seen on a mammal.

"This is incredible," Cerberus said. "Did you make this?"

"Sal, this is my son Cerberus," Leonidas said. "Cerberus, this is Sal."

"Sal VI, mind you," said Sal. "And it's obvious he's your son. The real question is, how did he get here?"

"I thought you were going to tell me how it can be possible that I haven't seen my dad in ten years, yet he hasn't seen me in twenty-five," Cerberus said.

"Sassy. Not enough sassy folks around here," Sal smiled. "Now, look. Your dad was eaten by the dragon, right?"

Cerberus nodded slowly.

"And then you waited at home for ten years, missing him terribly, right?"

"Hey!" Cerberus was offended. "I didn't just wait at home! I worked hard to get here."

"Shhh," Sal said. "We'll get to your story in a second."

"I don't know if I like you or not," Cerberus frowned.

"So, like I said, you're at home for ten years, missing dad. And then you pop through to here," Sal continued. "But you're missing a key detail, which is *when* did the dragon bring your dad *here*? And the answer to that is twenty-five years ago from when we are now. Ergo, to him you've been apart for twenty-five years, and to you, he's been away for ten."

"But how is that possible?" Cerberus was still confused.

"Because the portal you used didn't just take through space, it took you through time," Leonidas stepped in. "But the dragon can travel through both as he pleases."

"Time travel?" Cerberus said. "I don't believe it."

"If you ever get home," Sal continued. "Come back to this spot and dig. You'll find your proof."

"*If* we ever get home," Cerberus sighed. "So why did we end up here?"

"How did you get here, Cerberus?" Leonidas asked. "Did you really stabilize the portal?"

"No…" Cerberus said. "Ricky did. He fixed it, and then he found a spike in the energy indicating you were alive, so I came through to find you."

"Wait," Sal was on to something. "The king thinks you're valuable because he thinks you fixed the portal. Don't mention Ricky again. Let the king keep thinking what he believes is true, and we might have a chance."

"Is Ricky going to open the portal again?" Leonidas asked.

"Even if he did, he can't bring us out," Cerberus said. "He has no MonFus, so his portal could only move in one direction. MonFus is the only known substance that can open a portal that can move in both directions."

Leonidas's face fell.

"But he has a working portal," Cerberus continued. "And we know what the problem was with your original one. It was never your technology. The dragon was alerted by the use of MonFus and interrupted us. When Ricky sent me through, the dragon wasn't aware since we used a different type of energy to power it."

"So, once we get the portal here running," Leonidas said, "we may be able to connect to his portal, power it up remotely, and have a locked exit-point back home."

"Exactly," Cerberus said.

"But we'll need to power it with MonFus, otherwise we won't be able to navigate both time *and* space. Still, we won't be able to get anywhere using MonFus so long as the dragon lives. He'll always be in the way."

"So, we have to kill the dragon," Sal said.

Both tigers turned to him. For someone with no body, this was a strange contribution to add to the brainstorm.

"If we kill the dragon, you can get us home and close the portal before the king finds out," Cerberus said.

"Exactly," Sal repeated.

"How are we going to kill the dragon?" Cerberus asked.

"I don't know, but it's the only way."

"Then we'll need to find a way to study the dragon up close," Cerberus said.

He hoped nobody could hear the fear in his voice.

21

"This lab was established for Project A.R.C.H., a bridge between time and worlds."

Sal stifled a laugh as he clarified further. "A bridge between time and worlds *for the king's personal amusement.*"

"What do you mean?" Cerberus asked.

"Well, the king loves history. He's building the portal so that he can create a collection," Leonidas said.

"Basically, his own little museum consisting of something from every great moment in history that's ever happened," Sal said.

Cerberus looked over at the portal. "So, for all these years here you've only been building this portal?"

"Yes."

"The portal you built back at the ARL didn't take you anywhere near this long to complete," Cerberus said. "And now there are two of you working on this one and it's taken twenty-five years?"

Leonidas paused. "…Yes."

"So, why doesn't it work? Why haven't you come home?"

Leonidas took a breath and rubbed his neck slowly with his paw.

"Little one, you know as well as I do, if I had attempted to return home, the dragon would've followed and brought me back here again."

"So, does the dragon need a portal to travel?"

"No," Sal said. "It can travel on its own. But unless you're inside it, you're not going anywhere. The dragon doesn't follow time the way we do—it could vanish with something and drop it off five hundred years ago. It's here, not here… totally unpredictable."

"The portal works differently, though," he added. "It's stable. Just like the one you had back home. With it and the right power source, we can lock onto an exact destination."

Cerberus crossed his arms. "So then, why does the king need you?"

"He didn't know portal travel was possible," Leonidas replied. "At least until when we opened our portal at the ARL for the first time twenty-five—or, I guess, ten—years ago—who knows how many years from now—the dragon sensed the use of MonFus. So, once the king understood what we had done, he sent the dragon to bring me back here, because I'm the doorway to the technology he desperately craves to possess."

"His 'doorway to the future'," Sal said.

"So then, who are you in all this?" Cerberus asked, not meaning to be rude.

"I'm Sal," said Sal.

"No, I—what are you doing here?" Cerberus said, increasing his unintentional rudeness.

"I'm the king's 'doorway to the past'."

"Sal's been here as long as King Luridae," Leonidas said.

"Longer, even."

"And how long is that exactly?" Cerberus asked, frustrated. "You know, I've seen plenty of folks with claws, but I've never seen anything like him. And the way he talks, saying things like *I always have been and always will be,*' I guess I just don't understand. How long can he have possibly been king, whatever he is?"

"King Luridae is as old as the First Moments themselves," Sal said. "And me, well, when *I* came from, they called them the *Final Moments*."

Cerberus gasped, although he didn't mean to. When he was a kidden, he had heard fantasy tales about the beings, the *people*, from before the First Moments. But nobody had ever met one. They had all been extinct for thousands of years by the time Cerberus was born, and nothing remained of them but ancient and rarely seen fossils. Cerberus had only ever seen one in a traveling museum special exhibit on a school field trip. He still remembered it well, a casting of an assumed leg bone preserved in petrified amber. Nobody had ever recovered a full people skeleton, and most folks doubted that the amber casting was even real evidence that people had ever existed. In fact, many seedy collectors had been rightfully called out for falsely casting the bones of other animals in Amber, trying to pass them off as genuine people bones since so few knew the difference.

"Sal?" Cerberus began, unable to contain his curiosity. "If you're from before the Final Moments, have you ever seen a people?"

"A people?" Sal asked. "Little tiger, I *am* a people, a human, at least what's left of one."

"King Luridae has Sal's body locked away, somewhere hidden," Leonidas said.

"What?" Cerberus asked. "Why would he do that?"

"Well, it's not a regular body, mind you," Sal took a breath.

"I lost that during the Final Moments themselves. Fortunately, I was prepared with a back-up plan: a mechanical body, which I had been developing for years prior. But the king took it from me when I… I, myself, tried to kill the dragon. Ever since, he's kept it locked up, and me his prisoner … I couldn't even tell you how long it's been. It's been so long."

"The king keeps him here because he is the only one with true knowledge of the history before the Final Moments. And once the king has access to this portal, he'll be able to use Sal's knowledge of the past to influence and change it for his benefit." Leonidas said.

"But if we kill the dragon, the king will lose his way of controlling and intercepting the portals and we'll all be able to home?" Cerberus asked.

"Yes, exactly." Leonidas said.

"But Bernadina..." Cerberus looked at the floor. "Even if we can get this plan to work… if I leave, King Luridae will surely throw Bernadina into the incinerator as soon as he realizes I betrayed him."

"So, I presume, we have to get this Bernadina from the dungeon, kill the dragon, get my body, and *then* get through the portal, all before the king notices?"

The notes of sarcasm in Sal's voice were easily detectable.

"I'm sure we can do all of that, easily."

Cerberus took a deep breath. "Well, not just that actually, I need to get Northsie and Johnsto out of here, too."

"So," Sal balked. "You want us to rescue not one, but three folks from the dungeon, and —"

"Well, actually, Bernadina is in the only one dungeon, Northsie is part of the castle household staff, and Johnsto… well I don't know where Johnsto is. But he's somewhere around here I know it."

"How much trouble did you get into on your way over here?" Sal was flabbergasted.

"Wait…" Leonidas looked up from his work. "Johnsto Dubeck?"

"I think that's his last name, I'm not sure. Both he and Northsie came from Bismarthi."

Leonidas's face fell.

"Little one", he said slowly. "If the king has Johnsto Dubeck, he has him locked away under the strictest security. I don't think getting all of us out of here, including him, will be possible. As your father, I think we should focus primarily on getting *you* home and safe. You're not supposed to be caught up in this. If anything happens to you here, I don't know what I'll do."

As Cerberus took in his fathers worried face, he felt a wave of confidence wash over him, and stood firm.

"You don't know what I've gone through to get here," he said. "No matter what happened, I haven't given up. It hasn't been exactly easy."

"Cerberus," Leonidas said.

"And I'm not about to give up yet."

"I said, Cerberus!" Leonidas was stern.

"So why doesn't your portal work?" Cerberus slammed his paw on the table in frustration.

"This doesn't make any sense. You're smarter than this. You have ever tool here at your disposal, every material. You should be home by now!" Cerberus sank. He was exhausted. "You should've been home long before now."

"The king doesn't think our portal works," Leonidas said quietly. "It just needs a power source, like the MonFus we had back home, but we've never told him that."

"What?"

Cerberus paced over to the portal.

"The king's not exactly running out of time," Leonidas said. "So, we've just been making him wait."

"But why for twenty-five years?" Cerberus asked.

"To someone who has been around as long has he has, it only feels like a matter of minutes." Leonidas said.

"As far as the king is concerned, since I came here by myself, without alerting the dragon, I must have the knowledge of how to get a portal working successfully," Cerberus realized. "That's why he wants me down here working with you. To him, I'm the missing piece of the puzzle."

"Exactly." Leonidas said. "I've missed you dearly, but I didn't expect you to find your way here like this. Now if we're going to keep everyone safe, we need a new plan."

Cerberus looked at his father. Brainstorming and working together again felt strange, yet familiar and welcome. He wondered what their lives would've been like if the king had never sent the dragon to take him that night in the ARL, and what life would've been like if they had continued to work together researching and rescuing lost animals instead.

Since that fateful night, Cerberus had never thought he would have another chance to live life with his father again, and now suddenly there was a real opportunity being presented to him.

"Dad, if there is a single chance we can turn the portal on, properly of course, and get out of here, I think we need to take it," Cerberus said.

"If we wait a few days and then tell the king that Cerberus successfully got the portal working, we'll be able to earn his trust," Sal said.

"So, let's get the fuel and turn this thing on," Cerberus said. "Once the king sees that we're making progress, he will trust us. Then we can work on calibrating it specifically for our needs without making him suspicious."

"That's far too risky, little one," Leonidas said. "If King Luridae knows the portal is functional, he'll —"

"—He only needs to know that it's functional. He doesn't need to know it's complete," Sal interrupted.

Cerberus looked around the room at the charts and graphs on the wall. He needed to find something to use that was subtle enough to convince the king the portal worked, but not to the point that it was ready to be used at its full capacity.

"We need a proof."

Cerberus was surprised he remembered that detail.

"I have two," Sal said, tilting his head towards a cabinet in the back of the room. "I've held onto them for a long time. One for a buffalo, and one for a penguin."

"Let's bring back a penguin," Cerberus said. "Buffaloes exist here already, I've seen them. What would be so special about bringing back another, even if it's an older one?"

"You're right, a penguin is perfect," Leonidas smiled. "Bringing a small, unfamiliar creature back is perfect. That way we can tell the king that the portal functions but has a limited size capacity."

"We can tell him that we expect to have the finished version ready a week or so later," Cerberus said, feeling proud of himself.

"Then, while he's waiting, we'll kill the dragon and make our escape."

22

Cerberus calculated that if they could successfully win the kings trust by bringing back a penguin, they would have just about eleven days total to fully execute their plan. In addition to working on the portal itself, they would also have to rescue Bernadina, find Johnsto, convince Northsie to give up her oath to this new-found community, kill the dragon, and lead the entire group to safety, including his father, Sal, and ideally Sal's body, too—whatever that meant. Yet, as crazy as it seemed, Cerberus wasn't about to give up. Everyone here was counting on him, and he hadn't come this far in his journey just to leave someone who needed him behind.

The first step in the plan was to find a way to speak to Northsie outside the castle walls, somewhere safe and private. If she could be certain the king wasn't listening, maybe she would be more open to being convinced to join their escape.

Back in his room, Cerberus was hardly able to sleep. He tossed and turned with anticipation, wishing he had some sort of sleep aid. A calming tea would be nice. There were a lot of pieces to the plan, and he knew it was very important to stay well rested if he was going to do his best to pull everything off without a hitch.

Cerberus took a sip of water from his bedside and realized that there was one piece of the plan that they hadn't discussed, and that was *when* they should all return to. Cerberus and Leonidas had each gone through portals ten years apart, and who knew when Sal had come from? Cerberus had faith that they could turn the portal on once and escape together, but getting three folks to three unique times was an extra challenge that they would just have to figure out when they got there.

"I wish we had access to MonFus," Leonidas had mused. "I'm not sure what we can use as an alternative."

"Even if we did have MonFus, as long as the dragon lives it will sense our portal and pursue us endlessly," Cerberus reminded.

"Maybe there is a way to capture and preserve some of the dragon's energy before we kill it," Sal said. "In theory, we could refine its material to take advantage of its ability and create a two-way portal."

"I don't know how we get close enough to the dragon to take any samples without enraging it," Cerberus said. Then he got an idea.

"Wait…if the dragon is like a lizard, does it shed its skin? Does it molt?"

"I'm sure it does," Leonidas said. "Since it has scales, it must shed them periodically."

"But if the dragon exists outside of time, always here and never here at once, do the scales decay?" Cerberus asked.

"I suppose in theory, they just would exist in perpetuity," Sal replied.

"Wait." Cerberus said, putting two and two together. "That's why the dragon was able to sense our portal at the ARL, and every portal using MonFus."

"What do you mean?" Leonidas asked.

"If the dragon can sense the portals; it must be because its biomatter was used to power them. They're connected. That's why when Ricky used the bunny energy to power the portal that sent me back here, the dragon wasn't alerted. He didn't use anything from the dragon in his experiment."

"But, Leonidas, how would you have used dragon scales in powering your original portal at the ARL before you even knew about the dragon's existence?" Sal asked.

"The dragon's scales…" Cerberus said, "The blue scales! Dad, back at the ARL, the MonFus that you used was blue. But where were you able to find scales that far from now in the future?"

"I brought them back from a mining expedition in the mountains," Leonidas said. "I was alerted to a strange power source, and when I went to investigate it, I quickly realized it was exactly what we needed to power our portal to find different animals across all of time."

"The plateau with the portal that Maximo uses to dump secret waste from the castle," Cerberus said. "I've been there."

Cerberus explained the hole where he and Bernadina had seen Maximo and his guards pouring the secret bags of strange waste deep in the mountains.

"I can't believe I didn't recognize that blue glow sooner," Cerberus said. "But, if that place is just a dump for the dragon's scales, maybe we can retrieve some and use them to power our portal. Once we kill the dragon of course."

"The source of MonFus," Leonidas said. "I can't believe it, but the location and origin make sense. But here, I have no idea how to get there again, especially with the king, Maximo, and his guards always watching our every move."

"So, that would be the next step in the plan then," Cerberus said. "We'll find a way to retrieve the scales, and then we can combine the energy with the penguin proof and bring back a penguin shortly after."

Knock, knock.

Cerberus opened his eyes and sat up with a start, accidentally knocking over his bedside lamp as he unintentionally flailed his arms. Even with everything on his mind, at some point he must have fallen asleep, and judging by the light peeking through his windows, it was now morning.

On the floor, the metal lamp had broken. Cerberus tried to quickly push the separated pieces together again.

Knock, knock.

One small flat metal piece wouldn't fit back into place easily, so in the interest of time, Cerberus shoved it into his clothes to conceal it. He carefully pushed the rest of the lamp back to where it had previously sat, tossing a handkerchief over the missing section.

Knock, knock.

"Sorry, just waking up," Cerberus called out. "You can come in."

The door to his room opened. Northsie poked her head inside innocently, as Cerberus crossed the room, drawing attention away from the bedside.

"I've brought you breakfast."

The tray that Northsie pushed in on a cart was a wonder to Cerberus's eyes: an assortment of salads, pastries, and meats that he had never tried before. It was hard not to overeat.

"Do you want some? I'm happy to share," Cerberus said, gesturing for Northsie to join him.

"No thank you," Northsie said, "I'll have my own meal later in my quarters, once chores are finished for the day."

"I have some supplies that I'll need King Luridae to allow me to go retrieve," Cerberus said when he was finished eating. "If he authorizes it, I'd like for you to accompany me."

"That's kind of you, but I have too many castle chores," Northsie said as she put the dirty dishes back onto the cart.

"Besides, if you're trying to play a trick on the king, I don't want any part of it. I've sworn an oath to help to support and care for my new community, this castle, through the completion of daily chores."

"I'm only looking for assistance in bringing back some necessary materials for work we're doing at the king's request," Cerberus said. "You don't need to trick anybody. I'd bring my dad, but the king would never permit us to leave the castle together. I don't know who else to ask."

Northsie pushed the breakfast cart out of the room. "If you want me to join you, you'll need to ask the king yourself."

"I'd be happy to," Cerberus said with a smile.

***

Standing in front of the doors to the throne room, Cerberus wrung his paws together as he tried to calm himself. It was getting quite hot, and he couldn't tell if it was the presence of the king in the walls around him, or just his own nerves.

Slowly, the doors to the throne room swung open and Cerberus entered once again. As he approached the king's solid form, the molten red eyes cracked open, dripping tears of magma across the floor.

"You request my attention?"

"After working with my father and Sal, we have figured out how to power up the portal." Cerberus spoke with confidence.

The king's mouth stretched into a dripping magma smile.

"After one night, you've solved a problem twenty-five years in the making. I must admit, I am suspicious."

"We'll need to do a small test to make sure it's actually functional," Cerberus continued. "We'd like to start by bringing back a penguin. A small creature is perfect for our testing purposes. Once we can confirm success, we'll be able to calibrate the portal further and bring bigger things through it soon after."

King Luridae's torso fissured with steam as he sat up in his throne. He was already large, but sitting up straight, he towered over Cerberus more than the tiger had expected. The tips of his claws glowed red as they clicked with energy, and an excited magma tongue smacked against his cracked stone lips in excitement.

"What do you need to complete your test?"

"Well, you know how you sent the dragon through time to bring my father to you?" Cerberus said. "We think that, in theory, we could use energy from the dragon to power the portal. Maybe even something as straightforward as a few of its scales."

"And how were you able to figure this out?" King Luridae asked.

"My father didn't realize the level of power the dragon possessed," Cerberus said. "I only figured it out because of how I powered the portal I built to get myself here. My portal was nowhere near as powerful as the one that we are building for you, and my father hasn't been able to get your portal working because he didn't realize that the necessary power source has been here all along. He thought the power came from his, well… our, time—but actually it came from yours. From here."

"If dragon scales are all you need, this will be easy," King Luridae smiled. He snapped a claw in the air and Maximo quickly entered the room.

"You summoned me, my king?" Maximo said as he kneeled, sword in paw.

"Maximo," King Luridae growled. "Bring me some of the dragon scales."

Maximo raised his head. "The scales?"

"Yes, the dragon's scales."

"My king…" Maximo paused. "We don't have any scales."

Cerberus could feel the temperature in the room rise as the king's expression shifted into a displeased scowl.

"Not since we began disposing them after each molting period, my king, I mean," Maximo continued quickly. "We were afraid of the extended exposure. But we can get more next time the dragon sheds of course."

"I don't have time to waste, Maximo. I need them now."

Cerberus watched the stone floor of the room begin to glow red around Maximo's feet, the heat transferring into his basalt armor, causing it to glow as well. Maximo stayed bowed, but noticeably arched his back, grimacing in pain.

Cerberus spoke up. "Can't we just go and retrieve some from the dumping ground?"

"The dumping ground?" King Luridae asked as the temperature in the room went down a few degrees.

"Yes," Cerberus continued. "The night your guards found me and Bernadina, we saw them dumping some material into a hole on a plateau in the mountains. The particles were blue, I think they were dragon scales. If we can retrieve some of them, we could test them to see if they're a suitable source of power for the portal."

"And how exactly would you retrieve them?" King Luridae asked. "Maximo tells me they're toxic. Isn't that right Maximo?"

"Yes, my king." Maximo shifted his weight uncomfortably.

"I can't risk losing my most valuable researchers to toxic exposure," King Luridae said. "We'll have to find another way."

"Well, what if you sent Northsie with us?" Cerberus asked. "She's eager to help out with nearly any chores, and she's not a valued researcher. She could recover the scales on our behalf, without risking our exposure to the toxic elements."

"Why would you risk exposing your friend?" The king asked, his glowing eyes narrowing. "Unless you're trying to deceive me."

"Just like Northsie, my father and I are also sworn to support you and the needs of Cathorn, King Luridae. I only suggested utilizing her as she would be less of a liability in achieving your goals, and her help could enable us to get the portal up and running faster," Cerberus said. "But if you prefer to wait for us to find another way, or for the dragons next molt, that's no problem at all. I too would prefer not to risk her health. I'm here with my dad now, and that's the only reason I came in the first place. I'm in no rush unless you are."

King Luridae's eyes flashed white with frustration. Slowly, he stood and took a step down from his throne towards Cerberus. As he moved, drips of magma poured out of the cracks that formed in his endoskeleton, hardening again quickly.

"Maximo. Accompany Cerberus and the girl to the dumping grounds."

Now standing directly in front of Cerberus, the king extended a claw as he leaned in towards the tiger. The tips of Cerberus's whiskers singed in the proximity to such extreme heat.

"Retrieve some scales, prepare my portal, and bring me a penguin," he growled.

The king gripped Cerberus's shoulder and dragged the tip of his claw down slowly as smoke from burning fur and flesh filled the air. Cerberus stumbled back with a scream. He clutched the deep wound in his shoulder, realizing quickly that it had already been cauterized by the intense temperature.

"Please know that if you do anything to try and deceive me, the pain you feel now will be nothing in comparison to what I ensure will follow."

The heat surrounding Cerberus and Maximo dissipated instantly as the room plunged back into total darkness.

23

Maximo, Cerberus, and Northsie rode up the side of the mountain as the sun began to dip. As was to be expected, Maximo held the reins of the buffalo-pulled wagon, guiding its every move. Cerberus and Northsie rode in the bed, tied up and blindfolded.

Nobody was feeling particularly social, and it had been a quiet ride. The buffalo seemed to be in high spirits, stopping at two separate occasions to joyfully follow a butterfly and lick up a freshly fallen snowflake. Each time a buffalo became distracted, Maximo would shake the reins and give the respective buffalo a hard kick to get its attention back on the road. Maximo's kicks were strong, but thanks to their thick pelts, the buffalo remained seemingly unbothered.

"So, have you spoken to Johnsto since you've been here?" Cerberus asked Northsie, trying to sound as casual as possible.

Northsie huffed at Cerberus in response, as Maximo whipped his head around in fury. "How dare you mention that traitor's name here?"

"Oh. I didn't know that he was a traitor. I just figured if she was working in the castle, maybe he would be too," Cerberus said, adding, "He also cared deeply about chores and community."

"He did not care about community," Northsie spoke up angrily. "He endangered not only our community of Bismarthi by neglecting to properly care for the water tower but has also endangered this newfound community as well. King Luridae would never have him work in the castle, in fact, when I pledged my allegiance, the king told me he has him held in the deepest dungeon."

"Oh, yeah," laughed Maximo. "Part of his special collection."

Arriving at the plateau, Maximo beckoned for the buffalo to stop, and the three of them exited the wagon. Maximo carefully removed their blindfolds.

"Stay here."

Ahead, the familiar boulder stood. Cerberus and Northsie stood by the wagon, as Maximo approached it. He carefully dislodged the massive stone from its bed and rolled it to the side, opening the hole that had been plugged moments ago.

Cerberus turned to Northsie. "All right, so what I need is for you to reach in there and pull a couple of scales out."

"Do you have a suit or something protective for me to wear?" Northsie asked.

"Uh," Cerberus hadn't thought about that.

"You've got to be kidding," Northsie said, "okay, here I go."

"Wait," Cerberus said, "wait!"

Discreetly, Cerberus pulled the flat piece of metal he had taken from the broken lamp out of the folds of his clothing. He held it out towards Northsie, who raised an eyebrow of concern.

"When you pull out the scales, I need you to drop this in there," he whispered.

Northsie took the piece of metal and turned to Maximo.

"Hey Maximo, Cerberus wants me to drop this in the hole."

"What's that?" Maximo came over quickly, snatching the piece of metal from Northsie's paw.

"This piece of metal? No way. What are you plotting?"

"No plotting here," Cerberus stated with confidence. "It's just important that I put this in the hole too. I only asked Northsie since she was going over there already."

"What for?"

Cerberus thought fast, trying to think of an excuse that Maximo would be amenable to.

"For the magnets. It's a special component. Very important. If we put it in the hole, then the portal will be able to draw additional energy."

"What does that mean?" Maximo asked, confused. "I've never heard of a 'magnet'."

"Look. If you don't let me, put this piece of metal in that hole, I'll tell the king that the scales aren't toxic," Cerberus said quietly. "I'll tell him that I saw you and your soldiers applying the scales to your armor back when you picked us up. I don't know what those scales do for your armor, but I know that you've been lying to him. I don't think he would like to hear that."

Maximo put his paw on the hilt of his sword with a growl. "And then what happens?"

"Then you get exposed. But either way he'll send Northsie and me back here to put this piece of metal in the hole because I say it needs to be in there for the plan to work, and I'm the scientist," Cerberus said, "So, we can put this in here now, or we can put this in here later, but now seems easier in my opinion—for all of us."

Maximo stood silently, grinding his jaw in rage.

Cerberus turned back to Northsie. "All right, see, everything's going to be all right. We just need you to quickly fill a sack up with scales and put this metal in the hole. Don't worry, you'll be safe. It's such limited exposure. Then we'll head back to the castle, and you can keep doing your chores."

Sack and metal in paw, Northsie looked at the angry Maximo with hesitation.

"You may proceed," Maximo growled through his clenched teeth.

Northsie approached the glowing hole and carefully lowered her arm in, sticking the metal into the side of the opening. She then began to fill the small sack with glowing, pulsing scales.

"That's great Northsie," Cerberus said, "We should have plenty of scales in no time."

Northsie dipped her head into the hole as she pulled up more scales. Once she was out of view, Maximo spun around and quickly fired three hard punches into Cerberus's injured shoulder. Cerberus clutched his arm as he doubled over in pain.

"Don't ever disrespect me again," Maximo whispered, as he leaned over the tiger. He gripped the hilt of his sword and flashed a wicked smile. "Or I'll chop that arm off."

Maximo spat at the ground and extended his arm to help Cerberus back up, as Northsie emerged with her sack full. Maximo then rolled the boulder back in place over the hole and affixed the blindfolds to Northsie and Cerberus as they boarded the wagon once again to begin their journey.

"Is this really still necessary?" Cerberus asked.

"The entrance to the castle is to remain secret. You're lucky I don't bind your wrists," Maximo said, and the wagon departed for the castle.

***

Upon return to the castle the blindfolds were removed. Maximo sent Northsie on her way. He then took Cerberus back down the elevator to the lower-level laboratory.

"Next time I see you, you'd better have a penguin with you," Maximo growled as he pushed Cerberus back into the lab, slamming the door shut.

"How did everything go today?"

Leonidas put down his work, and Sal turned his head as Cerberus raised the glowing sack of scales proudly.

"I got the MonFus," Cerberus smiled.

"Here, let me take a look."

Leonidas took the bag and peered inside. The pulsating glow lit up his face.

"Well done, little one."

Leonidas took the bag over to some equipment. He removed some scales from the bag, placed them on a clear surface and began inspecting them closely. He took a long wand, connected to a wire, and passed it back and forth over the scales. The readout began to hum with each pass.

"My, this is incredibly powerful material indeed."

Leonidas took a scale and placed it inside of a glass bell jar. As the scale fell to the bottom, pulsing bolts of blue energy bounced against the glass walls like lightning from a Tesla coil. He and Sal watched with passionate curiosity.

"I wish I had my old UltraNine laser to calibrate this stuff properly," Leonidas said wistfully.

Sal and Leonidas continued their investigation and after some fiddling with mores lab equipment, the energy pulse seemed to slow and stabilize.

"My friend, I think you've done it," said Sal.

Paws shaking with nerves, Leonidas picked up the glowing bell jar, transferred the contents to a cannister, and—once sealed— carried it over to a platform near the portal.

"I think this is as stable as we're going to get this stuff. Shall we give the portal a try?"

"If you're ready, I'm ready," said Cerberus. "Let's bring back the penguin. What do you need me to do?"

Leonidas placed the humming MonFus cannister on the platform and connected it to some thick cables that lay nearby. The bulbs above the top of the portal began to glow slowly, imitating the same pulsing pattern displayed earlier by the scales.

"Alright, I'm going to connect the Penguin proof now."

Leonidas connected the proof to the device, and a faint red pulse flowed into bulbs, blending into the blue MonFus. However, unlike the time he'd done this to bring back Lupita, the MonFus' glow failed to turn its signature purple hue.

"What's going on?" asked Cerberus. "Why isn't the MonFus turning purple this time?"

"The proof must be too weak. The power from the scales seems to be overwhelming and absorbing it," Sal said.

"We need to find something to balance the power," Leonidas called over the sounds of the devices.

The red light faded as the MonFus overwhelmed it. Cerberus looked around the room, ready to try any possible solution.

"Hang on," Cerberus said, "Sal, since you existed at the same time as penguins, could we use you as an additional proof?"

Sal smiled. "That's a brilliant idea. If we can pull from my memories, we should strengthen the penguin proof and pull this off. Leonidas, this kidden really does take after you."

"He always did pay close attention back home," Leonidas said with pride. He gestured to some cables on another table across the room.

"Alright little one, connect those to Sal and let's get ourselves a penguin."

"Sal, do you mind?" Cerberus asked politely.

"Not at all," Sal replied. "I love a good ride."

Cerberus lifted Sal's jar and carried it over to the platform near the cables. At the base of the jar were two brass sockets, with a button in the center. Cerberus attached one cable to each.

"Go ahead, press the button," Sal said.

Cerberus did, and instantly the pulsing voltage traveled from the MonFus down the cables into the portal and into Sal's jar. His eyes rolled back and the little patch of hair on his pale head stood straight up in the liquid he was submerged in.

"Sal, are you okay?" Cerberus asked. But Sal didn't respond.

"Should I turn it off?" Cerberus yelled to Leonidas, across the room. "Sal's not responding!"

"No! The machine is using him to locate a time where he and penguins both co-existed. It's going to take a lot of power to connect him back to then." Leonidas replied. "Okay, Sal, I know it's been a while since you've seen one, but it's time to remember a penguin—

and remember it like it was yesterday!"

Sal moaned as red energy surged through him. Across the room the portal shuddered. Cerberus looked over at his father, manning the machinery confidently. He couldn't help but feel nervous.

"All right, here we go!" Sal managed to yell out above the crackling roars of the electrical pulses, his pupils vanishing as his eyes turned pure white.

Leonidas pulled down a lever, and the red lightning in Sal's jar surged and vanished, traveling rapidly down the cables to the portal, blending into the MonFus—shifting it from blue to a balanced purple. The device hummed loudly as Sal refreshed himself, refocusing his eyes and stretching his jaw.

The lights atop the portal glowed purple, and slowly, the doors began to crack open. Cerberus felt the room vibrate and shake, and his spine stung as he felt the presence of the dragon growing around him.

"It's here," he whispered. Even out of earshot, Leonidas knew what he'd said.

"Don't worry little one, it will be different than last time," Leonidas called back in assurance. "This time, we're doing this for King Luridae!"

The room shuddered as though the dragon understood. Yet, as the portal finished opening and the doors locked into place, Cerberus could see its form lurking faintly in the glow on the other side, as if it were challenging them to try and escape.

"Here it comes," Sal said, and Cerberus took a step back, this time ready to fight if necessary.

"No, not the dragon," Leonidas said calmly. "Cerberus, look."

A little silhouette was forming in the doorway of the portal, and with a pitter-patter of little wet feet, a medium-sized penguin came into being. Curious, it waddled out from the portal and into the room. Slowly, the portal closed, and the light in the room flickered back to normal.

Unfamiliar with these creatures and this environment, the penguin quickly turned around to go home, but since the portal door was now closed this wasn't an option. Leonidas approached it slowly, but afraid, it pushed itself back against the cold metal door.

"It's okay, my friend, you're safe here," Leonidas said, holding his paw out towards it. The penguin looked at the ground, nervous and unresponsive.

"Cerberus, come here."

On one paw, Cerberus was overjoyed that he and his dad had finally succeeded in their dream of working together to bring an ancient animal back without fail; but on the other, he felt sad for this penguin. Just moment ago, this little creature had been walking around his home, and now he had been pulled into a strange new world with nothing familiar in sight. It must be scary. It was clearly scary.

Would Lupita have felt the same way? As curious as Leonidas, Cerberus, and even Ricky had always been, maybe it was best for these animals to stay in their own time and place, where and when they were supposed to exist with their friends and families who loved them. Cerberus had always thought it would be incredible for the animals that had been lost to time to have another chance, but now, seeing the fear and confusion in the little penguin's eyes, he felt differently. Maybe this world wasn't a good place for them anymore. Maybe forcing these animals to become a part of it was a mistake.

Leonidas knelt before the penguin and flashed a warm, loving smile.

"I'm Leonidas, and this is my son Cerberus." Leonidas said, gesturing for Cerberus to kneel as well.

The penguin honked softly.

"It's okay, my friend." Leonidas asked.

"Dad, I think we made a mistake," Cerberus said. "I know we need him for our plan, but what happens to him after we make our escape?"

"When we leave, he's coming with us, too," Leonidas replied. "Nobody gets left behind."

"Great, as if this plan weren't already hard enough," Sal moaned from across the room.

24

"Well, well. I always knew that dragon was valuable in more ways than one."

King Luridae watched in amazement as the penguin waddled around the room, doing its best to avoid the molten cracks in the stone.

"I'll call him Herring," King Luridae said.

Herring honked.

"Cerberus, it's rather incredible that you've managed to get our portal working so quickly," King Luridae said, "Especially compared to how little progress was made before your arrival."

Cerberus tried to avoid meeting the king's gaze as Herring honked again. It was really a funny sound.

"With this landmark success, and the twenty-five years previously spent on developing and refining the process, I think it is only a fair expectation for any final adjustments to be done tonight so that the portal can be fully operational by tomorrow morning," King Luridae said confidently.

"Maximo and the young servant will be sent to retrieve more scales from the plateau tonight, and tomorrow morning at sunrise, we will activate our long awaited fully functional portal."

Cerberus glanced at Leonidas with concern; he'd had hoped that there would be more time to get the pieces of his plan in motion. But to do anything besides agree would arouse suspicion.

"That is indeed a fair expectation," Cerberus replied. "We'll be ready tomorrow."

What are you doing? Even though Leonidas didn't ask this out loud, the look on his face was obvious. Luckily, King Luridae was still too preoccupied watching Herring waddle around to notice.

"The young servant and I will depart as soon as she finishes her castle chores." Maximo said, having been present in the room for this entire exchange, albeit insignificantly.

"Excellent," King Luridae said as his mouth cracked into a smile. "You've all done good work. Tomorrow is when the real fun will begin."

"And we look forward to it," Cerberus replied. "This opportunity to continue the work my father started long ago is something we appreciate immensely."

"I do expect everything to go as smoothly as today has," King Luridae said. "Now, return to your lab to ensure that outcome. I may exist eternally, but I've never met a tiger who shares that gift. We wouldn't want to have to test your limits."

Maximo, Cerberus, Leonidas, and Herring exited the throne room as the magma dimmed to cold blackness once again. Once they were back at the elevator, Maximo went his own way, while the tigers and penguin returned to the safety of the lab.

"What happened up there?" Sal asked as they regrouped. "Did it all go well?"

"Cerberus, why did you tell him we could be ready by tomorrow?" Leonidas asked in exasperation.

"Because we *are* ready," Cerberus replied. "If we tell him there's another delay or problem, he'll be suspicious—and that's not good for any of us."

"You should've let me do the talking, little one." Leonidas said. I've made it through twenty-five years here, you just arrived."

"Well, the portal *is* ready," Sal said.

"I *know* the portal is ready. We need more time for the plan." Leonidas rubbed his forehead in frustration. "How are we supposed to pull off this endless list of rescues by tomorrow morning? We don't even know where half the folks we're supposed to be rescuing are."

"I think the king is already suspicious that we're trying to trick him. You were there when he was talking to us," Cerberus said. "Now that we've brought Herring back successfully, he knows we can do it. If we appear suspicious at all he is going to know."

"Your kidden is right Leonidas," said Sal.

Herring honked.

"Sorry, I just realized I don't know your actual name." Cerberus said, turning to the penguin. "I only know you as 'Herring' which the king came up with, not the name you showed up with. I didn't want to be rude."

Herring stared at Cerberus blankly.

"Sorry, I —"

Herring honked again.

"I'm just —"

Herring honked and ran around the room flapping his wings.

Cerberus looked at Sal and Leonidas.

"Wait, what's happening?"

"What do you mean?" Sal said. "He's just doing penguin stuff."

"I didn't mean to offend him," Cerberus said, "Why is he ignoring me?"

"He can't talk," Leonidas said.

"Why not?"

"He's an animal," Sal replied.

"I'm an animal, and I can talk," said Cerberus. "Right?"

"Right…" Sal said, "but animals from before the Final Moments couldn't."

"I don't get it," Cerberus was confused.

"So, you can talk, right?" Sal said. "But the buffalo who pull the carts and carriages can't. Have you ever wondered why?"

"I suppose I hadn't ever questioned it."

Cerberus looked over to Leonidas and back at Sal again. Though Leonidas's face was covered in fur, and Sal's was bare and pink, they had a lot in common.

"Alright little one, there is more that you should know," Leonidas said.

"What do you mean?" Cerberus asked.

"Well, the first thing is that King Luridae was created by the Final Moments," Sal said.

"Was he a people, too?" Cerberus wondered.

"No," replied Sal, "he was a scorpion—a tiny, black-shelled creature with claws, an arachnid. The only arachnid to remain after the Final Moments. The rest were wiped out instantly—but King Luridae, though we still don't fully understand why, was changed, becoming the being you met in the throne room."

"What do you think happened?" Cerberus sat down to listen.

"From what I understand, when the Final Moments occurred, King Luridae was at the direct impact point of a fission-based atomic disintegrative thermonuclear device, and in the explosion, his scorpion body absorbed flowing magma that had been released from below the planet's surface. This caused him to mutate and merge with the molten core of our planet. Everything I knew from my time appeared to be destroyed in a flash. Once the dust settled, he arose from the wreckage right here in would become known as Cathorn, sparking a new emergence of life in the area. That event, which happened thousands of years ago, is what you have been taught to call the First Moments."

"He raised his castle from the very lava that formed his body," Leonidas said. "That's why he's able to move through the walls with such ease."

"How did you learn all of this?" Cerberus asked.

"The king found me here in the wreckage," Sal said, "I lost my body in the Final Moments. As far as we know, I am the last known survivor of the human race."

"Strangely enough, the disappearance of the humans led to a change in the animals," Leonidas said, "especially the ones that lived on the edges of the destroyed areas."

"What do you mean, changed?" Cerberus asked. "How did the animals change?"

"It's hard to explain exactly, but they became more like people," Sal said. "And once the king learned I was a scientist, he used me and my knowledge to change the animals even further."

Leonidas pulled some old and weathered evolutionary charts off a shelf and spread them across the table for Cerberus to examine carefully. Each sheet showed the different evolutionary stage of each animal, tracking all their changes and mutations over the centuries leading up to the current era.

"Before the Final Moments, I worked with other humans in an animal modification lab, where we captured animals from the wild, and experimented on them, seeing if we could successfully infuse them with human traits so they could aid humanity," Sal said. "When King Luridae learned my history, he made me his prisoner and encouraged me to give all of the humanoid animals human minds, pushing the evolution further than it had ever been. I thought that we were rebuilding the world together, but really, he was just looking for more subjects to rule. Our work is why you're standing here today."

"I can't believe it," Cerberus whispered in shock.

"Over time, and under the king's watchful eye, the rising animal society built Cathorn—which evolved into a bustling city. Not long after that, folks ventured out in all directions, starting their own independent societies. That's where Bismarthi and the other villages come from. Yet, without access to my body, I've remained here as the king's prisoner, learning from nothing but whispers and passing shadows."

"I didn't realize humans had such a long lifespan," Cerberus said, "and without a body? Sal, how could you survive long enough without a body for the king to find you?"

"My research had predicted that a cataclysmic event like Final Moments was approaching, so I took initiative by preparing a way to preserve my brain," Sal said. "I transferred my head to an artificial body, one that wouldn't age, and would allow me to protect myself.

But, once our work was complete, the king separated me from my artificial body, and sealed it away. As long as I remain here, I am the king's prisoner. There is no way for me to escape without my body, and if I ever tried to build a new version, he would stop me immediately."

"How many others know about this?" Cerberus asked.

"Besides the king and me? Only the two of you." Sal said. "Everything in your future has come from here."

"It's why he wanted me to work with Sal to build the portal together," Leonidas said. "Sal is only the knowledge of the past, and we are the only knowledge of the future."

25

Though it was impossible to see the sky from the inside of the lab, Cerberus, Leonidas, Sal, and Herring knew the morning was quickly approaching. Still, there was a lot of preparation ahead and other important questions that needed to be answered.

"So how does the dragon fit into all of this?" Cerberus asked.

"Well, the dragon first appeared at the same time as the creation of the king," Sal said. "Though it may have existed before then, there is no true way to know. But we do know where to find it. When King Luridae raised a pocket of the planet's molten core to create this castle —"

"— he created a cold, dark home where the magma had previously been. And that is where the dragon lives, right?" Cerberus asked.

"Unlike the king, the dragon doesn't speak, which makes it very hard to know anything about its origins or purpose," Sal said. "But the dragon and the king have a very symbiotic relationship. They take care of and protect each other."

"Still, it's kind of ironic," Leonidas said. "The king controls the dragon but can't go near him. The heat from the king would destroy the dragon, and the cold of the dragon could extinguish the king."

"Maximo tends to the dragon whenever King Luridae needs," said Sal. "As thanks, the king has provided him and his unit of soldiers with special chitin armor made out of basalt, forged out of his very own cooled magma."

"Interesting…" Cerberus said, "When Maximo caught me and Bernadina on the plateau, we saw them rubbing the dragon scales on their armor. It seemed like there was some sort of special reaction caused by the two elements touching, but when we were in the throne room earlier, the king seemed to think that they couldn't be exposed to each other."

"Maybe Maximo knows something that the king doesn't," Sal said. "I didn't think that was possible, but if it is true, it could play into our favor."

"But what will it matter once we kill the dragon?" Cerberus asked. "I think it's time that we head down into the castle depths so we can figure out how to kill it."

"If you're ready, I'll show you the way."

Cerberus followed Leonidas out of the lab and down a stone hallway to a heavy set of double doors. Leonidas pushed them open, revealing a staircase descending into darkness. He held them as, Cerberus stepped through. It was much colder on the other side.

"These doors won't stay open on their own," Leonidas said. "But don't worry, I'll wait here until you come back."

"I didn't realize we couldn't go together," Cerberus said in hesitation. "Are you sure you'll be okay up here?"

"You're the one heading down a dark stairwell to find a dragon," Leonidas replied. "I should be the concerned one."

"Aren't you?" Cerberus asked.

"Just come back quickly. I'll be here."

Cerberus took a deep inhale, clenched his paws, and gave Leonidas a brief hug. He set off, and the doors shut slowly and firmly behind him, shrouding him in darkness. As he descended the seemingly endless stairwell the cold grew, becoming overpowering. Cerberus wished he had a flashlight or even a torch to help light his way, but anything bright and warm would risk upsetting the dragon. The danger was already high enough.

After what felt like forever, Cerberus reached the last step.

Stepping out onto unseen ground, he had to trust his gut that there would be no more stairs to walk down. He stretched his arms out, feeling each surface with his paws, taking slow steps, as he made his way through what could be either a hallway or large room. Slowly a soft blue glow came into visibility, from somewhere beyond this area, defining a corner of the space, and indicating the presence of an upcoming pathway. This deep into the cave, the blue light could only be caused by one thing.

Cerberus approached the glow, and turning the corner, the dragon was finally revealed. It slept curled up in a ball, each head flaring its nostrils slowly with each breath, as the glowing light pulsed in synchronization. Now, thanks to the light, Cerberus could clearly see that this wasn't truly a room; if anything, it appeared to be a vast cavern, one so sprawling and deep, it was impossible even to see the back or ceiling above.

This cave must be nearly as large as the castle, Cerberus thought as he shivered.

He looked at the dragon's head that had been previously injured. What had been a series of bad wound were now nearly healed. He noticed the skin of the dragon slowly sagging with its breath, peeling forward; it would molt again soon.

If this beast has been around since potentially before the Final Moments, there's no way a physical injury is going to be able to kill it, Cerberus realized.

Then something caught Cerberus's eye. Behind the dragon, a ladder was flatly mounted against a wall, only visible due to the small amount of glowing light reflecting off it. It appeared to ascend directly up, climbing so far into the shadows that he couldn't even see the top. Cerberus had assumed that the stairwell he had followed from the castle was the only path here, so where did that ladder go? Back up into the castle? Or somewhere else entirely? Either way, it was very strange.

The dragon sniffled and tilted one of its heads. For a beast that had done so many terrible things, it looked strangely cute in this peaceful state.

Observing a sleeping dragon wasn't providing as much information as Cerberus had hoped, so his thoughts returned to the mysterious ladder. Maybe, if he could get over to it, he could investigate further and hopefully learn something useful to make this dangerous journey worth it.

Carefully, Cerberus sidestepped around the gargantuan sleeping beast and made his way towards the far side of the room. Looking up the ladder from directly below provided no further clues as to what was up there, so slowly Cerberus began to climb. As he did, he could feel the temperature rise as the dragon's glow faded into shadow below.

Though he still didn't know where the ladder was taking him, Cerberus was pretty sure he was climbing up higher than the lab itself. Finally, his paw reached the top rung of the ladder, and he was able to pull himself up onto a ledge and looked out into the torchlit room in front of him. Across him, stretching to the far ledge, was a collection of items of various shapes and sizes. Dark, cold magma columns created a gothic nave-type structure, placing dividers between the various artifacts on display.

Cerberus examined the curious collection, finding that every item was completely unfamiliar to him. Masks constructed of wood with strange paint and faces; pottery with symbols of people making various action poses painted on; a large steel box with wheels and a glass window that looked like some sort of vehicle.

Cerberus walked down a row of paintings that each seemed pulled from a completely different era, in both style and mediums. It seemed like this space held something from every moment of history, even predating the First Moments. Yet, as old as so many items here must be, strangely, everything in the room looked nearly new. There was hardly an imperfection or layer of dust to be found anywhere.

Across the area, closer to the opposing ledge, Cerberus noticed a strange construct rising above the displayed items, and he made his way towards it. As he passed suits of armor, space shuttles, flat sheets of glass, and stone-carved wheels, he realized what — no, *who* — was at the end.

Johnsto.

His golden robes had been replaced with peasant's clothes, and each of his limbs were tied to a different side of a system designed to suspend him staring straight ahead into depths of the sinister museum. Though his head was held facing forward, it hung unconsciously. This could only be some sort of long-term torture device.

As quietly as he could, Cerberus attempted to detach Johnsto and lower him down to safety. The once majestic buck now looked weathered, tired, and strangely, much older. Still, he opened his eyes and looked into Cerberus's own.

"Cubbin," Johnsto smiled. "It's good to see you."

"What happened to you?" Cerberus asked. "You look different. Older."

"The king sent me on a few rounds through time with the dragon," Johnsto chuckled softly. "He's just trying to intimidate me, but don't worry cubbin, I'm alright. It's good to see a familiar face."

"I didn't know where you were," Cerberus said, "But I wasn't going to give up on you."

"He's got me chained up here staring out at the museum as a reminder," Johnsto said. "He wants me to remember that all through time, at every moment, he's always been there, and that's why I should let him reclaim his rule of Bismarthi."

Johnsto took a deep breath.

"But my grandfather, Alaine, left for a reason, and I will always support his decision. The folks of Bismarthi will never be led by a king. There will never be one leader. We have always been and will always be a community that supports and care for each other through the completion of our daily chores."

Cerberus admired Johnsto's resolve, and felt his own confidence rise from sheer proximity. The room even seemed to be warming.

"Where did all of this come from?" Cerberus asked. "I thought the king didn't have a portal that worked."

"He uses the dragon," said Johnsto quietly. "He's always been able to send the dragon anywhere through time to retrieve whatever and whoever he wants."

"But then, why does he need us to build him a portal?" Cerberus asked.

"Because then I wouldn't have to bring things *back*."

The temperature in the area increased rapidly, and the closest structural column seemed to shift and grow suddenly. Dramatically, King Luridae's eyes and mouth cracked through the solid layer, revealing living magma inside the stone structure.

Cerberus leaped back with a start.

"You're here!"

"Of course, I'm here. You're in my castle, and, once I have my own portal, I won't need the dragon's help again," King Luridae laughed. "I'll finally be able to leave this place. I'll be free to go everywhere and any-when, finally able to truly control the past and the future, even before the First Moments. Before I ever took this form or had this power. With the completed portal, I'll truly become unstoppable."

The temperature in the room rose even higher as all the other surrounding columns began to glow, filling with molten heat.

"Unfortunately, neither of you will live to witness it."

"You need to get out of here," Johnsto called to Cerberus.

"No!" Cerberus pleaded as he rapidly tried to free Johnsto from the system, avoiding the surrounding drips of magma. "I can't leave here without you!"

"You should be helping Northsie, cubbin. Bismarthi needs her more than they need me."

"Hey!" Maximo's voice echoed across the room, as he and his guards finished climbing the ladder. "Bring that traitor to me."

Cerberus didn't know what to do. The ladder seemed like the safest way down, but Maximo and the guards were in the way. His best bet was to surrender, and hope King Luridae hadn't figured out the rest of the plan. Cerberus sunk to his knees as Maximo strolled over proudly, quickly wrapping steel-cuffed chains around his paws. The surrounding columns cooled, returning to their original form, as the one containing the king's face continued to pulse.

"Silly tiger. You thought you could best me." King Luridae said. "But I know the portal works, and I already have your father and Sal.

You'll spend tonight in the dungeon, and tomorrow, we'll activate the portal, I'll merge with the system to take control, and once I have truly confirmed your irrelevance, I'll execute all of you."

Maximo pulled Cerberus back towards the ladder by his chains.

"You know what?" King Luridae said. "Tomorrow, If I'm feeling really good, after I execute you for the first time, I'll travel back to the past just so I can do it again."

The room glowed red, as King Luridae cackled.

"I was here one hundred and seventy million years before the Final Moments, and I'll be here one hundred and seventy million years after you're gone as well," King Luridae laughed. "There is no time without me. There never has been and never will be."

In a flash, the column went cold and lifeless as King Luridae's molten core shifted through the stones themselves, traveling back up into the castle above. The temperature quickly cooled as the column returned to its previous and natural state.

Cerberus looked back towards Johnsto, as the guards tightened the buck's restraints ensuring that he would remain suspended. Cerberus then tilted his head back towards Maximo, who lifted his sword in response.

"Stop looking at me," he growled, bringing the hilt of his blade confidently down on Cerberus's forehead.

Once again, everything went black.

26

At the time, being stuck in a carriage with Lucinda, Henry, and Stephenson for the slow cross-country ride home from Culinary School had felt like being in a prison. He had never spent much time with Henry, and Stephenson hadn't been born until after Cerberus already been away for several years.

Even though there were many faster options of travel available, Henry had chosen to book the carriage ride as he thought it would be good for Stephenson; an experience designed to give him *"the taste of the road"* and *"instill core values."*

So here Cerberus sat, trapped with a family that was his, yet also wasn't at the same time. He had just spent ten years running from his past, yet the moment he graduated; his past was instantly and aggressively thrust back on to him.

Henry B. Orenthall, the reminder of the loss of Leonidas sat directly in front of him, mere inches away. Whenever the carriage hit a bump in the road, Henry's hooves would bounce off the ground and slam back down on Cerberus's own paws. Unfazed, the boar started through the carriage window with glossy eyes as he explained the difference between terms like *"Postmodern Candidian Nouveau"* and *"Racontent Heritage Modernism"* to six-year-old Stephenson.

The carriage hit another bump in the road. Cerberus winced as Henry's hooves came down on his own paws once again. "Sorry, lad," Henry said, "I know it's a tight squeeze, but when you see how good Stephenson turns out, you'll know it was all worth it."

"He's right," Lucinda agreed. "We all need to support Stephenson during this important learning phase."

All Cerberus could do was nod and look out the window silently, finding a tree or post moving in the distance to focus on for long as he could.

The journey was thirty-four days long and two birthdays were celebrated during. One was Stephenson's, and the other was Henry's. Lucinda had packed surprise gifts for each. Both verbally expressed disappointment that Cerberus had not done the same.

At the end of the ride, as they pulled up the driveway of their home, Cerberus made a mental note that a stay in prison couldn't possibly be worse than that.

***

However, as Cerberus came to consciousness and attempted to rub the sore spot on his head, only to find his paws had been restrained to the walls by a short length of chain, he began to question whether he may have been wrong in that assumption.

He hadn't expected to be caught so quickly. None of the plan had been going smoothly and even if the king's proposed test went well, there was still a high chance Leonidas would be deemed worthless and executed—not to mention the many others who would be put at risk afterward due to the king's megalomania.

Cerberus thought about his poor mother, and all that she had lost. He thought about Ricky, waiting for him with his portal in a time that Cerberus would much rather be in. A time that seemed less and less likely to ever be able to return to. The future felt bleak, and as Cerberus finally opened his eyes, he saw Bernadina chained up by the old bench on the other side of the cell — and remembered how much this adventure had cost her as well.

"You sure took your time getting back here, I see," Bernadina said bitterly.

"I'm doing my best, as quickly as I can."

Cerberus tried to stand, but the chain binding his wrists were too short.

"What do we do?" he asked as he sunk down again.

"Nothing. And thank you for it."

"Thank you? What do you mean?"

"Before I met you, I had already lost my family to King Luridae, and now, because of you, I'm going to lose my own life as well. So, thank you, Cerberus. Of all the inns in Cathorn, I'm so glad you walked into mine."

"Bernadina, I —"

"You left me here. I didn't have much, but I risked it all to help you find your father. The moment King Luridae had Maximo drag me away, you let me go and never came back. You didn't even say anything when he did it."

"What was I supposed to do? He's literally made of living magma!"

"You could've protested. You could've said you needed me. You could've — I don't know…" Bernadina hung her head, wrists bound to the bench in the back of the cell. "I just thought…"

Bernadina took a stuttered breath.

"Since you had put so much effort in to save your father, Johnsto, and Northsie, I just thought you would put in a little more to save me as well. Instead, you just tricked me into helping you for nothing but your own gain, and then abandoned me at your first opportunity."

Cerberus's heart sank.

"Bernadina, no," he said, "I never forgot about you. Rescuing you was always part of my plan. I just never got the chance to say it."

"How am I supposed to believe you?" Bernadina asked. "Of course, you would say that now that you're chained up in here with me again."

"Please believe that I never meant to abandon you, Bernadina," Cerberus said, "I couldn't be more grateful for your help. Without you, I never would've found my father."

Bernadina lifted her head slightly. "You found him?"

"Not only him, but the others too, Johnsto and Northsie," Cerberus said. "So, all we have left to do now is kill the dragon and get everyone through the portal before King Luridae catches us again. And when I say everyone, that includes you."

"Kill the dragon. Escape through the portal. Got it," Bernadina replied. "However, I think you're forgetting one thing here."

Bernadina swung her arms back and forth. The chains attached to her wrist clanged loudly.

"What are we going to do about these?"

Cerberus smiled. "Can you reach under that bench?"

"Why?"

"If you trust that I'm going to keep my word to get you out of here too, please try." Cerberus said.

"Fine."

Bernadina bent down and found the chains were just long enough to reach under the bench. She felt around lightly.

"Yeah, I guess I can. Now what?"

"There should be something under there."

Bernadina moved her arm back and forth, suddenly stopping as she felt something unseen with her paw. Quickly she glanced around to check for any nearby guards and once she confirmed that none were in sight, she retracted her arm held up the flat piece of metal that Cerberus had previously stashed under the bench.

Cerberus couldn't help but crack a smile.

"You put this here? When? How?"

"Before," Cerberus said. "I found it after they patted us down at the plateau, but it's a long story. The dragon-scales dumping spot where we met Maximo seems to be some kind of timeless portal-hole-thing. I stashed that piece of metal inside it when Northsie and I went back to retrieve some scales, but I pulled it out *before* that, back when you and I were there ourselves the first time and was able to hide it in our cell when I was imprisoned in here with you on our arrival. Do you think you can use it to help us get out of our chains and this cell? Maximo is away right now with Northsie on a mission to gather more scales. If we leave before they come back, we may still have a chance."

"That's not that long of a story," Bernadina said, as she slid the metal into a tense area of her chains. She gave the metal a hard twist and the chains snapped open in an instant. "But it is ridiculous one."

"I thought you weren't going to believe me."

"Well, things can't get any worse for me, can they? So, I may as well try to make everything better for everyone else."

Bernadina hopped off the bench and stood, stretching.

"So why are they out getting scales exactly?" she asked as she fiddled with Cerberus's chains.

"Basically, the portal needs them as its power source. In the morning, King Luridae is going to test the portal. If it works, he's going to kill all of us and then take over all of time."

"Oh okay, sure," Bernadina said. "That sounds like something we're prepared to handle."

The metal shackles on the tiger's wrists clicked open, and Cerberus stood up, letting the blood return to his sore arms once again.

"All right, what now?"

"Now we go rescue Johnsto and kill the dragon," Cerberus said.

Bernadina inserted the metal piece into the dungeon cell gate latch, and after a moment of wriggling, the heavy iron door swung open.

"Great, I'm glad you have this all figured out," Bernadina said. "So, what will we need to do in order to kill this dragon?"

Cerberus looked at her, as concern flooded his face.

"I have no idea."

27

Cerberus and Bernadina quietly made their way down the cold, damp hallways of the dungeon. They were careful to stop and peer around each corner and doorway to avoid being seen, and finally they found themselves back at the door to the lab.

Cerberus raised his paw. Gesturing for silence, he placed his ear against the cold door. On the other side, he could hear Maximo's guards talking to Leonidas and Sal who were now working under close supervision.

"Maximo will be back with those scales soon," a guard was saying with what sounded like a mouthful of taffy. "So, make sure this thing is ready when he is."

"Yeah," said another guard. "King Luridae won't want to wait."

"Why is any of this good for you?" Leonidas asked, disdain dripping from his voice. "Why are you so devoted to helping him?"

"What's good for King Luridae is good for all of us," the guard replied. "When he gets what he wants, we all benefit."

"Well, good loyalty is hard to come by," Sal said with a lazy chuckle.

"I wish you had a body so you could help me with this heavy stuff," Leonidas grumbled. Cerberus could hear what sounded like a large steel pipe being dragged across the room.

"This is the first time I'm happy King Luridae took mine from me," Sal joked. "The king got what he wanted, and I'm definitely benefiting right now."

The guards chuckled.

Cerberus pulled his ear from the door and gestured to Bernadina that it was time to keep moving. As they continued down the hall slowly, the temperature grew colder. Cerberus felt his spine tingle as they approached the heavy doors that separated them from the stairwell that would lead them down to the dragon's domain.

"Once we get down there, you'll see the dragon," Cerberus whispered. "And behind the dragon, across the room, you'll see a ladder. Climbing that ladder will lead us to Johnsto. He's trapped in something, but —"

"Can't we kill the dragon first?" Bernadina interrupted. "Wouldn't it be easier to kill the dragon, then save Johnsto?"

"If we kill the dragon, King Luridae will sense it. And if the guards notice we're missing from our cell, King Luridae will be alerted. Either way, the first thing he'll do is make sure we have no chance of getting Johnsto out," Cerberus said. "We need to rescue Johnsto first, and then kill the dragon. In that order."

"Got it," Bernadina nodded.

Cerberus pushed the doors open slowly. He remembered how the last time he had been here, Leonidas had promised to wait on the other side for him. Cerberus looked forward to a future where doors and portals wouldn't keep them apart any longer.

Bernadina and Cerberus made their way down the stairs, descending into the cold and damp cavern. Cerberus knew what to expect upon reaching the bottom from his last visit, but as they turned the corner Bernadina couldn't help but let out a barely audible gasp. She quickly covered her mouth to quiet herself.

In front of them, the glowing dragon slept comfortably, its blue glow pulsing with each breath. Slowly, it shifted its weight, settling into a new, seemingly more comfortable position, and let out a gentle snore—one that might have been considered adorable coming from a smaller, less dangerous creature.

Cerberus placed his paw on Bernadina's shoulder to get her

attention, and gestured to the ladder across the room, behind the sleeping beast. Bernadina nodded in confirmation. Carefully, the two made their way around the dragon, and once they reached the bottom, began to climb. As they ascended, the dragon faded into the darkness below.

During the long and silent climb, Cerberus thought about how excited he was for the day to come that he would never have to see another portal again. He couldn't wait to return home with his father and convince Ricky that the concept of the ARL was an inherently flawed one.

The sooner all portal technology can be destroyed, the better.

Cerberus reached for the next ladder rung, but his paw grabbed at empty air. They had finally reached the top, and Cerberus once again found himself in King Luridae's underground vault.

Bernadina pulled herself up from the ladder and joined him in looking around. "So, this is the king's personal museum," she whispered.

"Different objects from the past, all collected here," Cerberus replied. "And once King Luridae has his functional portal, he won't need any of it anymore. Now follow me, Johnsto is down this way."

Cerberus started moving with caution but turned around to find Bernadina holding back. He watched as she peered down the various aisles with interest and curiosity.

"Bernadina, come on," Cerberus whispered with urgency. "It's not safe to linger here."

"But Cerberus," Bernadina said, "don't you want to know what else is here?"

Transfixed, Bernadina started to slowly explore an aisle, taking in the many various artifacts forged from stone, wood, metal, and advanced technology.

"We could learn so much about history from these objects," she continued as she stared in awe. "We could use them change the world."

"We can't risk anything right now," Cerberus said. "We need to get to Johnsto."

With a look of forlorn longing, Bernadina heaved a heavy sigh as she turned back to continue with Cerberus. Together, they made their way towards the back of the cavernous underground museum, and soon they found Johnsto, suspended and restrained, exactly how he was when Cerberus had left him last.

The once proud buck slowly opened his eyes and raised his head as they approached.

"Cerberus, you came back?" Johnsto whispered.

Cerberus and Bernadina looked over the bindings that held Johnsto suspended.

"We're all getting out of here," Cerberus said, "and that includes you."

"Where's Northsie?"

"We're getting her next," Cerberus said.

"How do you know the king isn't watching you again?" Johnsto asked.

"I don't. But even if he is, I'm not giving up on you."

Bernadina kept watch as Cerberus twisted and pulled at the bindings that held Johnsto, but nothing seemed to give.

"I can't get them open."

Cerberus continued to twist the bindings, harder and harder, his frustration growing. Finally, he let go, sinking down to the ground in shame.

"I can't do it," he said, "the restraints are too strong."

"Cerberus," Bernadina said, "maybe there is something here that can help.

Cerberus turned towards the endless rows of artifacts.

"Alright. We need to find something that can help us break these bindings, and quickly," Cerberus said.

"I'm on it," said Bernadina.

Johnsto watched as the tiger and racoon explored the aisles, turning up various objects, taxidermy, and even petrified plants—yet nothing appeared to be suited for this specific task.

"We're running out of time," Bernadina said quietly. "The longer we spend down here, the more likely it is that they're going to realize we're missing."

"We're not giving up Bernadina. Northsie needs him. Bismarthi needs him," Cerberus paused. "I promised them I would get him home. Just keep looking—there has to be something in here we can use."

"If we can't find something soon, we need to leave," Bernadina urged. "Johnsto will understand. I know the Dubecks understand loyalty. They're famous for it."

"I already told you; we're not leaving him. Or anyone."

"Cerberus, I know—"

"Wait!"

Something had caught Cerberus eye.

"I don't believe it!" Cerberus said as he approached what appeared to be a display pedestal featuring small, tube-shaped item with a softly glowing diode tip.

"My dad's old UltraNine!"

"What?"

"An UltraNine laser can cut and reseal molecules on an atomic level," Cerberus said quietly. "If anything can get Johnsto out, this can."

The tiger reached forward in excitement, but Bernadina quickly grabbed his arm.

"Careful," she whispered. "It may have an alarm."

Cautiously Cerberus kneeled, lowering himself to the height of the UltraNine laser display and blew gently. Slowly, the device began to roll off its perch. It fell, and Cerberus caught it swiftly without making sound. He and Bernadina stood frozen for a moment, waiting to see if anything would happen, and when it again felt safe, the tiger couldn't help but to twirl it around in his paw like an old familiar friend.

"My dad always told me that with this tool, anything was possible," Cerberus said with a proud smile. "He called it 'The Creator's Pen.'"

"How do you know it's your dads?" Bernadina asked. "The king could've acquired it anywhere."

"Oh, I would recognize this anywhere." Cerberus rolled the UltraNine around in his palm. Engraved at the bottom of the handle was a single letter: *L.*

"My dad had it when he was taken. Leaving it in his possession would've made him far too powerful for King Luridae's liking, I'm sure."

Cerberus gripped the tool with pride and confidence as he approached Johnsto's bindings once again.

It took a little calibration, but the UltraNine did the trick, just as Cerberus knew it would. The bindings fell to the ground, and Johnsto lowered his arms for the first time in who knew how long.

"Where's Maximo?" The buck asked. "We don't want to get caught like last time."

"He's off on an errand for the king," Cerberus replied. "Getting us the fuel we need to power our portal. The portal we're going to use to get out of here."

"Very smart, cubbin."

Johnsto did a few quick stretches, and some of the life returned to his face as his body recognized that it was now truly free. Cerberus and Bernadina jumped to follow.

"No reason to spend any more time in here than we have to," Johnsto said as he started making his way back towards the ladder. Cerberus hurried to catch up as Bernadina followed.

"Hey Cerberus, mind if I keep this?"

Cerberus turned around to see Bernadina holding a magnificent sword with a broad golden saber and a large purple gem laid in the hilt. She twisted a switch on the grip, and the blade suddenly sprung apart, forming three jagged blades.

"My dad used to give me lessons," she said with a smile. "Never with a sword this cool, but I think I can figure my way around this one too." Bernadina confidently clicked the three blades back into the neutral singular saber position.

"You do seem to be figuring it out quite quickly," Johnsto chuckled. "And sorry, but I haven't yet caught your name."

"I'm Bernadina," Bernadina whispered.

"Hi Bernadina," Johnsto said. "I'm Johnsto."

"Wait!" Cerberus whispered urgently. "Over here."

Cerberus approached the first row of items in the museum.

"I didn't notice before, but these items are much dustier than everything else in here," Cerberus whispered. "These must be the first items that were placed here back when the king created this museum."

A shuddering sound grabbed the groups attention, and they noticed that just slightly down the row an unusually large crate sat, enforced with steel chains and a heavy lock. On the top corner a dusty readout flashed between dim red and white lights. Gently, Cerberus nudged it with his paw, and it shuddered again.

"It looks like there's a label."

Cerberus used his sleeve to wipe a thick layer of dust off, revealing the text underneath. Though extremely faded and faint, the markings seemed vaguely familiar.

"Hey, I think this is Sal's body," Cerberus said. "His body was one of the first things the king stored in his collection, so it would only make sense for it to be here at the front row."

The box shuddered again, as if in response.

"Who?"

"Oh right, you haven't met Sal yet."

"Cerberus, I don't know why somebody's body would be in a box, or how anyone could live without one, but I do know that every moment we linger around in here is a moment that makes us more and more likely to be caught."

Johnsto was getting impatient.

"We need to get out of here before the guards return."

"Okay," Cerberus said. "I just need a second."

Cerberus pointed the UltraNine at the crate's lock and twisted the setting.

"And I promise this makes sense."

Cerberus clicked a button on the UltraNine's handle. The tool emitted a thin beam, and the lock slowly separated into two distinct pieces as the chains relaxed. The faint readout went dark.

"What are you doing?" Bernadina whispered furiously.

"Something I promised I would." Cerberus replied. "And you know I'm big on keeping promises."

The crate held still for a moment, but then the top popped open with a click. Still, nothing emerged.

"It's okay, we're here to help," Cerberus whispered.

Slowly, two long metal arms cautiously rose out of the crate. Cerberus took a step back.

"Metal?" he wondered aloud. "But people aren't metal."

Johnsto and Bernadina stepped behind Cerberus as he raised his UltraNine laser slowly.

"Is it possible you made a mistake, cubbin?" Johnsto whispered.

With a graceful bounce, a metallic form with eight long, hinged, sharp, legs leapt from the crate, landing directly in front of Cerberus. Slowly, Cerberus twisted the UltraNine laser, expanding the beamwidth. He didn't know if it would work as a weapon or not. Bernadina raised her golden sword.

"Cerberus, move," she growled, stepping in front of him.

But the robotic figure wasn't here for a fight. Quickly it turned away from the group, jumping, and scurrying almost silently down the hallways until it reached the wall at the far side. Upon reaching it, the legs bored into the stone, and it began to climb, up and up, until it finally disappeared out of sight into the darkness of the chasm above. Cerberus, Bernadina, and Johnsto watched in silence.

"Cerberus," Johnsto began, "I know you're a tiger with a good heart who always looks out for his community. I trust you know what you're doing, even if I don't understand it. And this is something I definitely do not understand."

"What he said," Bernadina declared in hesitant agreement.

"I promise I'll explain later, but we've really got to go."

"Oh, so *now* we're in a rush," Bernadina snorted.

One after the other, Johnsto, Cerberus, and Bernadina made their way down the ladder and back into the dragon's cavern. As the glow pulsing around the still-sleeping beast came into view, Johnsto had to pause admire it.

"I've never seen it this clearly before," he whispered with reverence. "It's kind of magnificent, isn't it? At least when it's peaceful."

"So can we kill it now?" Bernadina asked. Her eyes grew wide as she gripped the handle of her newfound sword.

"Tomorrow morning, before king tests the portal. That's our chance," Cerberus replied. "We need to kill the dragon as close to our escape as possible to minimize the risk of the king catching on. If the king knows the dragon is dead, then we're all guaranteed dead, too."

"You told me we'd kill the dragon after we found Johnsto," Bernadina grumbled.

"And we will," Cerberus replied in whisper. "But the timing is everything."

After some careful maneuvering, the three companions found themselves safely past the dragon and back at the long stairwell. They began climbing up the steps slowly, already out of breath.

"So, I take it that you found your father?" Johnsto asked between breaths.

"Yes, and right now he's completing work on the portal I mentioned. The one that's going to get us all out of here."

Johnsto stopped on the steps and turned to Cerberus to give him a warm hug.

"I'm so happy for you, cubbin!" he said as he wrapped his arms tightly around Cerberus. "I knew you had the strength to do this."

A flood of emotion washed over Cerberus's face.

"Thank you Johnsto," he smiled back. "I've been so concerned about making sure each step in this plan goes right, I guess I haven't taken much time to appreciate how far I've already come."

"Well don't slow down now," Johnsto replied, "We're almost at the end."

Cerberus paused for a brief, but necessary, moment to smile and take a deep breath. He nodded proudly at Johnsto as he turned to continue up the stairs.

"You're right. We're *almost* at the end—but not there yet," he said, "Everything hinges on tomorrow morning. We need to be completely prepared and ready by the moment the portal test is performed. If the test is successful before we're ready, King Luridae will kill all of us immediately. We still need to find Northsie, kill the dragon, and be ready to escape with my father, Sal, and Herring all before the king turns the portal on."

"Who's Herring?" Johnsto asked.

"The king's pet penguin."

"Well okay then." Johnsto said. "I don't know what any of that means, but if you say we need to rescue this 'Herring' too, then you have my support."

"Bernadina and I need to get back to our cell in the dungeon before anyone notices how long we've been gone," Cerberus said.

"But we can't hide you there," Bernadina noted to Johnsto.

"That's all right, don't worry about me. I'll go find Northsie."

"Are you sure?" Cerberus was concerned. "Forgive my judgement, but you still look weak. It's my fault you're here, and it's my responsibility to keep you safe."

Johnsto threw back his head, jovially summoning a low, yet confident laugh from deep in his chest.

"The only thing ever to beat me in a fight was that dragon. I think

I'll do all right up here in the castle. You two get back to your cell. I'll find Northsie. I'm not just baggage on your adventure, I pull my own weight, don't worry about me gentle cubbin."

It felt like forever, but finally the group had reached the top of the stairs. The heavy set of doors were sealed fast, just as Cerberus had expected. Without hesitation, he pointed the UltraNine towards the lock, and began calibrating the beam—but out of nowhere, Johnsto pulled him back, beckoning quietly to wait.

Cerberus pocketed his laser and learned forward slowly. Through the door, he could make out the sound of someone breathing heavily.

"Could it be Maximo back already?" Bernadina whispered. "Some sort of ambush?"

"Things have been rather quiet this whole time," Johnsto mused. "Suspiciously so."

"Wait." Cerberus placed his ear firmly against the door. "It sounds like someone crying."

Cerberus raised his paw to knock.

"Cerberus!" Bernadina hissed, "Don't risk everything on this!"

"This door is the only way we know out of here, Bernadina," Cerberus replied. "Either we cut our way through the door and risk making so much noise that we get caught immediately, or we rely on the kindness of whoever is on the other side to open it. They could be a friend."

Bernadina grunted in reluctant agreement. Cerberus took a breath to gather himself, shut his eyes for a moment, and upon opening them, gave the door one single, gentle, knock.

The breathing on the other side of the door stopped. But nothing happened.

Cerberus knocked again.

Bernadina raised her sword in nervous preparation.

The latch creaked, and slowly the door swung open, casting a beam of dim light across Cerberus, Johnsto, and Bernadina. It gleamed off the sword in her paws, and as she lowered it, the figure who had opened the door came into clear view.

Leonidas.

Immediately he wrapped Cerberus in a warm hug.

"You're back. You're back. I can't believe it," Leonidas breathed heavily in relief. "And you found your friends."

"I think I found Sal's body, too," Cerberus said.

"I can't believe you're all right." Leonidas's eyes welled with tears. "I was here watching the door for you when I heard the soldiers coming. I had to run back to the lab to avoid getting caught. Later, I snuck upstairs to check your cell, but it was empty. I feared I was too late. I thought… I thought… I thought I had lost you again. Again, I couldn't be there when you needed me. I'm sorry, Cerberus."

"You did what you had to do, and don't worry, we're all right. The king has no idea what we're planning." *I hope,* he thought, but didn't say that part aloud.

"He's been very focused on preparing the castle for the activation," Leonidas said.

"Have Maximo and Northsie returned with the scales yet?"

"Not yet. The king anxiously awaits their return."

"We need to hurry back to our cells, but we'll find you before the portal activation tomorrow," Cerberus said. "And then we'll make our move."

Leonidas stepped back. He smiled at his son proudly.

"Cerberus you really have grown up to be quite the tiger."

"But dad," Cerberus said. "I didn't do it without your help."

Cerberus held out his paw, revealing the UltraNine laser to Leonidas's awe.

"My old UltraNine! I don't believe it." Leonidas exclaimed "I'm so happy to see that it found its way into the right paws."

"But it's yours," Cerberus was confused. "Don't you need it?"

Leonidas wrapped Cerberus's paw closed around the laser,

refusing it.

"This UltraNine was always meant to become yours, Cerberus." he said. "Keep it safe—with this tool, your creativity will know no limits."

"I love you, Dad," Cerberus said, blushing under his fur. "I don't ever want to miss a chance to say that again."

"I love you too little one," Leonidas replied. "But I believe in you, and I know there are going to be many more opportunities to say it."

As the group passed the doorway to the lab, Leonidas slipped back inside. Soon, Johnsto, Cerberus, and Bernadina arrived back at the steel elevator. Cerberus and Bernadina stepped inside, but Johnsto turned to continue down the hallway on his own.

"My grandfather used to say the castle was full of secrets and tunnels," Johnsto said with a twinkle in his eye. "So, let's see what I find while waiting to recover young Northsie."

"I can see the spirit of Alaine Dubeck flowing through your veins," Bernadina said.

"True community isn't just those who are actively grouped around us," Johnsto replied, "True community includes those who paved the way for us, as well as those who we are paving the way for. We'll meet again soon."

As the steel elevator doors slid closed, Cerberus and Bernadina watched Johnsto go. Arriving back at the dungeon level, they sneakily returned themselves to their cell. Bernadina hid her new sword under the bench, out of sight. Cerberus made quick repair of the cell latch, fusing the broken pieces back together with the help of the UltraNine.

"You're getting pretty good with that thing," Bernadina commented.

"I had a good teacher," the tiger replied.

"I know I've been giving you a hard time," Bernadina said as Cerberus latched her both back into her shackles. "And I'm going to keep doing it until I'm safely back in my own home with all of this behind us."

"I know," Cerberus couldn't help but chuckle as he pocketed his UltraNine and slid his paws back into his own shackles as well.

"But you did a good job getting Johnsto out of there today," she said.

"*We* did a good job getting Johnsto out of there," he corrected.

Both the tiger and racoon couldn't help but smile as they settled back into their prison.

Now it was time to wait.

28

It was a shorter wait than expected. Hearing activity down the hall, Cerberus opened his eyes. Somehow, in this uncomfortable cell, the night before the most important morning of his life, he had successfully managed to fall asleep. Rescuing Johnsto had been more exhausting than he had realized. Bernadina looked over at him. For her, it seemed that sleep hadn't come so easily.

"Somebody's coming."

Down the hall, a commotion sounded—keys jingled—and a guard burst through the door into the dungeon.

"Please, please, please, let me figure this out before King Luridae hears about it," the guard mumbled to himself as he stumbled toward the cell holding Cerberus and Bernadina.

"Ah, good, you're both here," he said, breathing a sigh of relief.

"Of course we're both here. Where did you expect us to be?" Bernadina replied coldly.

The guard fumbled for his keys as he turned to called back down the hall from where he had come, "The prisoners are accounted for!"

Cerberus tilted his head towards the ground to avert his eyes as the guard fiddled further with the cells lock. He was clearly having trouble unlocking it.

Had the UltraNine laser reattached all the lock's components properly?

Cerberus held his breath, but luckily, the key worked. With a click, the cell door swung open loudly. The guard entered, oblivious to Cerberus's sigh of relief, drowned out by the squeaking hinges. He hoisted Cerberus up by his shoulders and began patting him down.

"What's happening?" Cerberus asked, wincing at the pain flowing through his injured arm. "Is something wrong?"

"Gotta do pat-downs," the guard replied, gruffly. "A prisoner has gone missing. Some contraband as well."

"A prisoner is missing?" Cerberus feigned concern. "Is he dangerous? It didn't seem like there was anyone else here in this dungeon with us."

The guard's frantic paw slid carefully dangerously close to Cerberus's concealed UltraNine laser, yet in his hurry, he concluded that his pat-down had been good enough and put Cerberus back down. The guard then moved on to Bernadina, repeating the process.

"The missing prisoner wasn't being kept in this—" The guard stopped, catching himself. "Wait, you're a prisoner. You don't need to worry about any of this, and I don't need to tell you anything."

"Thanks for the massage," said Bernadina.

Satisfied with his investigation, the guard locked the cell door once again, disappearing down the hall as he exited the dungeon.

Alone once again, Bernadina turned to Cerberus. "He must be talking about Johnsto," she said. "What are we going to do?"

"We can't do anything. But, if they're still looking for him, it means he hasn't been caught yet—that's a good thing," Cerberus said. "But, if we leave this cell, we'd be putting everything in jeopardy."

"I don't like the idea of leaving him out there, wandering the castle, all on his own."

"Johnsto's capable. I spent a lot of time with him in Bismarthi. He wouldn't want us to risk everything either—not when we're so close."

"Look," Bernadina said, "I'm not saying you're doing anything wrong. I'm just saying I would do things differently."

"Alright Bernadina," Cerberus huffed. "Should your friends and family ever be at risk, and I hope they never are—if I'm still here to help, we can do things your way."

The next several hours passed slowly as the tiger and racoon waited in silence.

Cerberus watched the shadows stretch across the room. He thought about his mother, Lucinda, at home in the distant future. Even though she wouldn't be born for a very long time, he knew that eventually the day would come when both he and Leonidas would be forced to abandon her, and that after that incident occurred, she would miss them both terribly. Cerberus was determined to return to his own time as closely as he could to the minute when he had left—that way she wouldn't have had to wait for him for too long, if even at all.

Without warning, the stone floor began to rumble. Cerberus felt the temperature in the cell rising. The mortar between the cracks in the wall began to sag as it turned bright orange and molten. King Luridae's voice echoed through the cell as the walls shifted.

"It's time."

Pushed up by a molten magma flow, the floor of the cell began to rise, lifting Cerberus and Bernadina towards the ceiling.

"Cerberus, the room is going to crush us!" Bernadina called in fear.

Yet, the mortar between the stones above them turned molten as well. The stones shifted away, clearing a pathway for the floor to continue to rise. Cerberus's injured shoulder brushed against a wall, the tips of his fur singing on contact.

The materials of the castle walls adjusted and rearranged, turning and interlocking like a massive three-dimensional puzzle.

"What's happening?" Bernadina called across the cell.

"I have no idea," Cerberus replied, "It feels like the castle is changing. We're being moved!"

"I think it's stopping," Bernadina said.

With a deep, low rumble, the structure found its new form and locked into place. Cerberus and Bernadina looked around their rearranged holding as the stone cooled.

"The door is gone," Cerberus said, "There's no way out."

"What are we going to do?"

The words had barely left Bernadina's lips when the walls shook in an instant response. With loud cracks, the walls fissured and lowered themselves into the ground, and as the dust cleared, Cerberus and Bernadina found themselves no longer in their cell. They were still chained, same as before, even down to the stone cell bench next to them—but, where they were was now entirely different. Even though the castle had adjusted its shape and design, becoming something unfamiliar, they could still recognize that the room they were now in was one they'd visited before.

The Throne Room.

The room had nearly doubled in size since Cerberus had last seen it. Newly formed narrow windows at the top of the walls allowed a small amount of light to leak through, casting thin beams of warmth across the floor as morning began. With more natural light illuminating the space, Cerberus could finally see that the room had the feel of a warped Gothic cathedral, with a large nave decorated with columns along either side.

Opposite from the doorway, on the far side of the room, the new portal stood ominously, complete, and magnificent. Sal's head sat on a platform near the portal as Leonidas worked on final adjustments and preparations. Two guards stood at the ready, fully concealed in the familiar chitin armor, carefully observing. Cerberus tried to stand, but quickly was reminded of the chains that held him in place.

"Finally, we're all here."

The ground rumbled again. From between cracks in the stones, heat and light began to gather. Molten magma seeped through the ground, swirling around as it took the standing form of King Luridae—legs, torso, claws, and even his scorpion-like tail. A final swirl took the shape of the kinds head, and as the magma quickly hardened, light cracked through the form of the king's head as his eyes and mouth sparked to life again.

The king took a slow and calculated step towards the portal, his leg cracking out of the previously cooled form, turning into magma once more, and cooling again on impact with the ground. He took another. Then another. With each deliberate step, the king shifted, heated, and cooled again, molten material cracking and dripping with each motion. He looked at the portal with admiration as he paced around it, inspecting carefully.

"Well, well, maybe all that time spent was worth it," the king muttered to himself. "It seems you have done your job quite well."

"Thank you, King Luridae," Leonidas replied, keeping his head low, careful to avoid eye contact.

"How long until we're ready to proceed?"

"Should be any moment," Sal said.

At the other side of the room, the doors opened. Maximo and Northsie entered, followed by two more guards carrying large containers that could only be full of MonFus.

"We have the materials requested," Maximo stated matter-of-factly, as the guards set them near the portal. Passing Cerberus, Northsie turned away as the slightest look of shame crossed her face.

"Where is Herring?" King Luridae asked, shifting his look towards the guards. "He mustn't miss this."

"I'll fetch him now," Maximo replied.

As Northsie helped Leonidas load the MonFus into the system, Maximo ushered the little penguin into the room and towards the king.

"Watch carefully, Herring," King Luridae said as the penguin waddled around the room, curiously taking in the situation, while simultaneously trying to avoid the heat.

"It is time for history and me to stop living side-by-side," King Luridae declared. "Today, I become one with both the past, and the future. Today, history becomes me, and the concept of time takes new form. Finally, things will forever be as they always should have been."

As the last container of MonFus was connected to the portal,

Maximo lead Northsie over towards Cerberus and Bernadina.

"Your work is done," Maximo growled. "Now you too will wait here and watch with the others. We shall have no interference with today's proceedings."

King Luridae's eyes flashes as the floor where Northsie stood turned molten and shifted up, forming a cuff around her ankle, restraining her. She winced, trying to bear the intensive heat against her flesh.

"Leonidas. Sal."

King Luridae's voice boomed through the room. He stood in front of the portal, the structure framing the space around him like a timeless portrait.

"Begin."

With no other options, Leonidas took a breath and flipped a lever. A burst of powerful electrical energy surged as the portal roared to life.

Color washed over the room as cracks of light and energy whipped back and forth, pulling in the power around them. The portal began to glow and swirl, forming the doorway that Cerberus knew all too well. Transfixed by the sheer power and opportunity, King Luridae's eyes began to glow. His mouth salivated, dripping with glowing hot molten magma.

He took a careful step forward, cracking and reforming the solid shell around his molten core. Each foot melted into the ground, creating a merged stability as he approached the portal with pride and confidence.

The king reached out his claw as energy ripped the shell off it, exposing his burning liquid core. He smiled as he watched his particles lose their gravity, swirling around him with a weightless energy. His eyes and mouth glowed even brighter as cracks of energy tore across his entire surface, rendering him into a completely molten mass. His core burned with heat.

Leonidas picked up Sal's head, and the two of them stood between the other two guards, as far from the heat as they could manage.

"I can feel it working. I can feel the energy flowing through me, becoming me," King Luridae yelled as the walls of the castle pulsed with heat in response. "It's almost time."

Transfixed, Cerberus watched the portal as it filled with power. The energy flowed through the king, the blue color turning to brown mud, pulsing with bolts of electric green. The king's eyes had turned a pure and bright white—and he appeared to be nearly frozen in his focus, overwhelmed by the surge of energy.

"Cerberus," Bernadina hissed quietly.

Focus broken, he glanced over at her.

"Now or never."

She nodded back in return.

"Never is now."

With the grace of a seasoned professional, Cerberus flipped the UltraNine out of his pocket, and with a quick adjustment of the beam, cut both his and Bernadina's chains open, unnoticed. He wrinkled his nose at Bernadina, and she blinked back in response, eyes darting towards the portal. Under the bench next to her, Cerberus could see her fingers wrap around something carefully.

Now it was time for Northsie's. Cerberus didn't know how she would respond, but there wasn't time to waste. Cerberus aimed his UltraNine at the cuff around Northsie's leg. He could see and smell the burned skin and hair from where it had formed around her.

"GO!" Cerberus yelled, releasing the UltraNine's beam. It sliced through the cuff on Northsie's leg as he sprang forward, scooping her up in one smooth motion. Maximo turned as Cerberus fell back, pulling Northsie out of his reach. As they rolled back away from the guards and towards the back of the room, out of the corner of his eye, Cerberus could see Bernadina, leaping swiftly from the floor, pulling something out from under the adjacent bench.

The golden sword strobed with light as it moved through window beam to window beam raised high in Bernadina's arms as she charged ahead.

Though she stumbled at first, Bernadina quickly grew in confidence and grace as she navigated around the swirling, burning liquid mass of King Luridae, dodged two guards, and with unexpected precision leapt into the air, grabbed the sword's hilt with both paws, and swung it into the structure of the portal.

At first it seemed to lodge and stick there, but Bernadina kept her paws on it, pushing it through the machinery. The golden blade started to turn red from the heat exposure to the energy, and the purple gem in the hilt began to glow. Energy from the portal cracked out like lightning, flickering from King Luridae to the gem—the gem seemingly growing more powerful with each flash.

With a sharp grip, Bernadina twisted the handle, releasing the split blade into its three distinct pieces. They cut through the rest of the portal's structure like butter. The light and energy flow disconnected and instantly vanished as the structure of the portal collapsed into useless, broken pieces strewn across the floor.

"What!"

King Luridae's eyes snapped back to their usual white with orange edges and his body of magma returned to its normal anthropomorphic form and began to cool again as he snapped out of his trance amidst the chaos.

The king looked at the shattered portal in front of him and locked eyes with Bernadina.

"No!"

The racoon raised her sword and stared at him, her eyes sharp and unyielding. There was not an ounce of fear to be found as she said, "You had my family thrown in the incinerator. You knew this was coming."

Bernadina charged, raising the golden sword, and reversing the twisted handle, merging the three blade segments back into a single, intimidating, one. Now charged by the hilt gem's energy stolen from the portal, unknown levels of power flowed through the blade, trembling to be released.

"Not today, rat."

King Luridae growled and flowed back swiftly, collapsing into a puddle of instantly molten magma. He vanished between the cracks of the stone ground, leaving no trace behind. Bernadina's powerful swing collided with the stone floor, sending out a rippling wave of energy upon impact.

"Arrest these traitors!"

Maximo yelled as he struggled to find his footing having been knocked back by the radiating wave. Cerberus, who was still carrying Northsie stumbled to regain his balance as well.

"Northsie, are you all right?"

"What's going on?" Northsie asked, worried.

"It's all going to be alright," Cerberus reassured her as two guards charged at them, weapons drawn. Cerberus raised his UltraNine, but before he could release the beam, one of the guards quickly knocked the other out of the way, leaving him unconscious.

Confused, Cerberus pointed the UltraNine towards the remaining guard. The chitin armor did seem very powerful. It was time to find out if this beam worked on everything.

"Cubbin, wait!"

The guard removed his helmet, waving frantically. Cerberus couldn't help but to smile when he saw who was underneath.

"Johnsto!"

"I caught one of these guys earlier," Johnsto said with a hearty chuckle. "And now I'm about to catch some more."

With no need for a disguise any longer, Johnsto proudly dropped the rest of the armor to the ground, revealing his glowing golden robes underneath.

"Found these rags in lock up," he said with a wink. "I think I'll keep them."

"Buck! You are wanted for treason in the name of Alaine Dubeck," Maximo bellowed across the room. "I'll see you returned to your prison."

"I hope you're not going to miss this one, cubbin." Johnsto said as he lowered his head. "In communities name."

Antlers pointed, Johnsto charged at Maximo aggressively. Maximo expertly stepped to the side, grabbing Johnsto's antlers as he passed. Quickly the two were locked in battle.

As the remaining three guards charged at Bernadina, Leonidas quickly picked up Herring, pulling the young, scared penguin out of harm's way. "I'll keep you safe," he said, comforting Herring's scared honks and flapping wings.

The ground began to rumble and shift.

"The king must be coming back!" Cerberus yelled out. "Be ready."

Bernadina readied her sword for another swing.

"This isn't the king," said Sal.

Cerberus shivered as his spine grew suddenly cold. The guards cowered, backing off quickly as rumbling from the front of the room grew violent. Stones began to slide, but not from being rearranged.

From being pushed.

Blue energy flowed into the room as the two-headed dragon rose from the ground. Pieces of the castle collapsed as it climbed up from the depths and into the throne room, exhaling steam from its nostrils. Both of its heads stared down at them in intimidation. Fully molted, healed and refreshed, any trace of previous injuries were impossible to find.

Northsie took advantage of the distraction by running toward Leonidas and Sal to seek safety in the familiar, while Johnsto used the moment to deliver a firm punch to Maximo's face. The leader of the guard fell back as Johnsto looked up at the dragon with a newfound rage.

"You want me?" he growled, as he looked between both sets of eyes. "You want my community?"

The dragon licked its lips. It seemed to understand clearly, displaying a mocking smile as it let Johnsto finish.

"This time, I'm ready."

The dragon charged. Jumping back, golden robes flowing, Johnsto ran, leading the dragon on a chase through the massive throne room, weaving through the columns and structures as the dragon dragged its body and second head behind, locked in cold pursuit.

"Surround the traitors!"

Maximo waved his arm towards the other guards and pointed at Bernadina and Cerberus. The tiger and racoon moved closer together as the guards approached, until they were back-to-back against the wreckage of the portal. Bernadina gripped her powered sword tight while Cerberus fiddled with his UltraNine's handle.

Maximo and his guards unsheathed their swords as they closed in. Spotting the spilled container of MonFus scales at his feet, Maximo stopped to pick some up confidently.

"You think you know power?" He laughed.

With passion, Maximo rubbed the MonFus across his armor. Quickly, it began to glow with energy, fusing the power of the magma that created it with the cold, timeless energy of the scales that were being used to power it. The other soldiers followed suit, and their armor began to glow bright blue, with a frosty steam emanating from it.

"You know nothing of power." Maximo snorted. "Our armor, this castle, the dragon, our king—your king. They are power, we are power. You are nothing but a peasant out of time and place. It's time for you and that rat to give up on all this trouble you're causing and turn yourselves in to face judgement for your terrible crimes."

"Never is now."

Cerberus pointed his UltraNine laser directly towards Maximo, releasing a powerful charged beam. Maximo shifted his weight, but the perfectly aimed blast hit him directly in the chest. He froze, but only for a moment as the beam reflected off his steaming armor, destroying a nearby structural column instead.

Across the room Johnsto spotted the impact and ran towards it, narrowly passing under it swiftly as it collapsed the stone ceiling upon the back of the dragon as it followed. The beast shrieked loudly as it shook the rubble off and continued its pursuit of Johnsto.

"Yes!" Leonidas called from the side. "Well done."

"We'll have all you traitors soon enough." Maximo said as he laughed and swung his sword at Cerberus who ducked out of the way. Instead, Maximo's steel blade collided against Bernadina's golden one, letting out a metallic clang louder than Cerberus had ever heard. Maximo scowled, stepping into his push, but Bernadina pushed back, holding her own. Cerberus didn't know what that sword was made from, but regardless of material, Bernadina had been trained well. He watched Bernadina gracefully swing her sword, defending from attacks on each side, carrying herself in a way that seemed effortless yet exhausting. She handled herself better than the guards did.

If this works out and I get home, I really need to practice self-defense more often, Cerberus thought.

"I just want to go home," Northsie sniffed as tears rolling down her cheeks. "To my real home. Can you take me?"

"You've stayed strong kidden. And we will get you home." Leonidas said, as he placed a paw on her shoulder in comfort. "But if we're going to make it there, you'll need to stay strong a little longer."

"Leonidas, without the portal, how are we going to get you and Cerberus out of here?" Sal asked his lab partner from the back of the room. "Maybe you can join these others back in Bismarthi. It sounds like a pretty nice place from what I've heard."

"Sal, are you alright?" Leonidas responded. "Something is happening."

With a soft flicker, the lights on the containment device used to preserve Sal's head began to turn on, and realizing this, he looked around curiously, both in confusion and excitement.

"Impossible." He whispered.

Up at the top of the throne room, through one of the narrow windows, a familiar shape arose. A metal form slid in through the window, dropping into the room next to them. Something mechanical and spider-like.

Sal's body.

"They really did it," Sal said, in quiet disbelief.

"When my little one says he's going to do something, there's no stopping him," Leonidas said with a smile.

"Let's see if I still remember how to work this thing," Sal said. "Alright, up—up. Come on."

In response, the body kneeled and extended its arms lifting Sal's head into the air and setting it down between its shoulders. Quickly, wires extended, and the two elements fused, becoming one cohesive mechanism once again.

"Oh, it has been a while. Got to warm up a bit."

Sal stretched his mechanical arms and legs. They clicked and whirred in response, calibrating with each new movement.

"It's time for me to do the carrying for once." Sal said embracing Leonidas and Northsie in his newly found arms.

"What—how are you—just stop them!" Maximo yelled in rage as he turned to see Sal leap into the air. It was incredible to how strong the pistons on his mechanical legs were. In one incredible motion, Sal soared across the room, carrying both Northsie and Leonidas up and out through the window to safety.

Furious, Maximo slammed his sword against a column. They were gone. He turned back towards Cerberus and Bernadina fuming with rage.

"Until just now, I was going to arrest you," he said. "But now, unfortunately, I'm afraid that's not going to be enough. Kill them."

Seizing the opportunity, one of the guards quickly swung his sword at Bernadina. She deflected it, her sword colliding directly against his steaming basalt armor. It stuck like a magnet, pulling steam towards the gem locked within its hilt. The guard looked down in curiosity and confusion. Bernadina looked up at him, and with a quick, sheepish smile, tried to pull the sword off again. It was stuck. The guard laughed and raised his own sword, ready to strike a direct and fatal blow.

Thinking fast, Bernadina twisted the handle of her sword, and the blade split into three once again, one blade piercing right through the guard's armor with ease. The guard screamed as his lifeforce seemed to vanish, instantly wasting away as if he had never existed to begin with. Besides a wisp of frosty smoke, nothing was left behind. The gem flashed and energy ripped out of the two other fragments of the blade, instantly evaporating the other two nearby guards as well. Three empty sets of chitin armor fell to the ground. The steam cooled, pulled along with the wisps into the gem at the hilt. It glowed softly as whispers of their screams held in the air for another moment before fading away into silence.

"Well, that was something." Bernadina said, feigning nonchalance as she reverse-twisted the handle, returning her sword to the singular golden blade.

"I mean, that's one of the most shocking things I've ever seen," said Cerberus, "and I've seen a lot of shocking things."

Still Bernadina was a great actress. She turned back to face Maximo, who was also doing his best to act as though he was unfazed.

"Your turn," she growled. "Murderer."

"I didn't kill your family, I want you to know that before you die," Maximo smiled. "I'm surprised you didn't figure it out sooner. They just abandoned you like everyone else."

"You're scum and a liar," Bernadina said, "If everyone in the world was like you, I would consider myself lucky to have been abandoned."

"Don't worry, I could never abandon you." Maximo said as he charged at her, blade drawn.

Maximo was clearly a much better swordsman than his soldiers, and he matched Bernadina's swings with ease, never letting the blade come close to grazing his infused armor.

"I won't make the same mistakes they did," he said, "But I'm sure you'll make a few of your own soon enough."

With a hard stoke, Maximo knocked the golden blade out of her paw. He kicked it across the floor and out of reach. He then lifted his sword, preparing for a powerful finishing blow, but stumbled as the ground below him gave way. The dragon's second head climbed up into the room, mouth agape. Maximo and Bernadina leapt away, both in opposite directions. As Maximo struggled to find his footing, he dropped his sword. It rattled over the rumbling stone, until it finally came to a rest against a wall on the other side of the room.

Crashing through a crumbling doorway, Johnsto burst back into the room, pursued closely by the dragon's open mouth, tongue flickering closer and closer. Still, his plan seemed to be working. The dragon's long body was getting tangled in a web between the narrow columns, hallways, and collapsing walls of the castle. Without the king to repair or rearrange the space, the options for the dragon's mobility were quickly becoming few and far between.

"Where's Northsie?" he yelled. "The castle is collapsing. We need to get her out of here!"

"She's safe!" Cerberus called.

"Wonderful! Okay get ready to run!"

Johnsto lowered his head and charged antler-first through each of the remaining columns around the room, shattering them one by one. As the stone ceiling collapsed around the dragon, its motion became even more limited. Suddenly, Johnsto pivoted to face the dragon's second head, which sat mouth open and ready.

"Johnsto!" Cerberus called out. "Let's go!"

"Protect our community," Johnsto called back, looking Cerberus in the eyes as he planted his feet confidently into the ground. Johnsto redirected his eyes, locking them with the dragon's second set. Behind him, the first head approached through the doorway, hungry to end this chase.

"In communities name," Johnsto whispered firmly, pushing off and into a strong, fast run. He lowered his head, leading with his antlers, deliberately running directly at full force into the dragon's second mouth.

"Johnsto, no!"

Cerberus couldn't believe what he was seeing.

Hungry and irate, the first head rushed at Johnsto, who continued to push himself further into the dragon's second mouth, aggressively tearing its throat with his antlers as he continued moving forward. Without hesitation, the dragon's first head charged into its own second mouth, instantly shredding it into ribbons upon collision. Still in focused pursuit of Johnsto, the first head pushed further and further into its own second throat, without even realizing what it had done. Flashes of light, energy, and smoke rose up from the continuing carnage.

Shrieking in pain and unable to see outside of its own throat, the dragon began to writhe violently against the walls of the castle, as if it was consciously trying to bring the whole thing down upon them. As it moved, its scales glowed bright blue, and the dragon began molting and re-growing them over and over, faster, and faster, quickly turning into nothing more than a shuddering blur.

With only a few support beams and load bearing walls remaining, the upper levels of the castle began to crash through the ceiling. Stones smashed into the ground, opening an impossibly deep cavern with each new collision.

The floor began to give way. The dragon's massive weight and vibrations were causing it to sink faster with each second. The chasm across the room was widening rapidly. Bernadina could see Maximo struggling to grab something at the edge of the widening gap. Finally, Maximo lifted his arm and waved something. It flashed purple. Enraged, Bernadina scrambled towards the edge. Cerberus extended his paw, stopping her.

"No. We have to get out of here."

"What about Maximo?" she shouted. "He has my sword!"

"Bernadina! The whole place is coming down!" Cerberus yelled. "We have to go!"

"I need my sword!" Bernadina yelled. She shoved off Cerberus's paw and pushed her way through the rubble. "You can get out of here. Your family needs you. I need to get *him*!"

"No!" Cerberus pulled her back from the chaos. He kneeled and looked directly into her panicked eyes.

"I'm not leaving here without you."

An unexpected calm washed over Bernadina, and her anger seemed to have been replaced by a new sense of peace. She paused to think for a moment.

"Okay," she said. "You're right. Let's go."

Cerberus breathed a sigh of relief. He couldn't help but to glance over at the few pieces that were still visible of the destroyed portal;

so many years of work, gone in a moment. Together, he and Bernadina turned away from Maximo and the wreckage, sprinting down the closest hallway, looking for any possible exit. Walls shattered around them as they ran, and cracks of light from the day outside showered through. Bernadina spotted something shiny in a corner—Maximo's sword! Loud cracks sounded up from the floors as she scooped it up and kept running.

"The foundation is giving way!" Cerberus yelled. "The whole castle will be fully collapsed soon!"

"There's no exits." Bernadina called. "Everything is blocked!"

"That way!" Cerberus yelled as he pointed at a damaged wall directly in their path.

"But that's a wall!" Bernadina called. "What do you want to do? Run through it?"

Cerberus was picking up speed. He showed no signs of slowing down.

"Alright. You're lucky I trust you." Bernadina said.

Cerberus shut his eyes, leaned into his good shoulder, and the two of them ran at the nearest crumbling wall as hard as they could. Without solid structural support, the stones gave way with ease. Bernadina and Cerberus stumbled through the rubble and into the castle courtyard.

"You made it, thank goodness."

Leonidas extended an arm to help them stand and gather their senses. Sal, Northsie, and Herring stood nearby, cautiously avoiding the destruction around them. Northsie's eyes rapidly darted around the castle, scanning every possible opening.

"Where's Johnsto?" she asked.

The fading screams of the dragon tumbling into the bottomless chasm provided the only answer. The color from Northsie's face drained as she collapsed to her knees in tears.

"No!"

Cerberus put his arm around her in comfort.

"If not for Johnsto's sacrifice, none of us would be here now," he said softly, "This was his choice."

"We need to get out of here," Sal said. "The castle is still crumbling, and as soon as the dragon is truly gone, the king will surely return to finish us off."

"But where are we supposed to go, Sal?" Leonidas said. "I've never been outside of this castle."

"And Bismarthi is too far away," Cerberus said. "It would take weeks to get there."

"I know a place," Bernadina said. "But we need to move now."

Cerberus ran to a buffalo-drawn carriage across the courtyard. Still tied to the hitching post, the buffaloes were panicked, trying to escape the chaos of the surrounding wreckage. Cerberus gestured for everyone to join and unhooked the reins as the group climbed on to the wagon.

"Let's go."

The buffalo didn't need to be told twice. With a crack of the reins, Cerberus led the wagon through the castle's courtyard gates, and the group sped down the snow-covered hills, making their escape. Rays of distorted blue light and bursts of electricity bled up through the rubble and faded into the sky as the last spires of the castle crumbled into the mountaintop being them.

Soon, only dust remained where the king's treacherous monument had once stood.

29

Hooves pounded as the buffalo pulled the wagon through the narrow streets of Cathorn. Leonidas, Northsie, Sal, Bernadina and Herring clutched the sides, holding on for safety. Cerberus cracked the reins, guiding the buffalo carefully. They were surprisingly nimble for such bulky creatures.

"Nice sword," Northsie said as she admired Bernadina's acquisition.

"I had to get myself a little trophy," Bernadina laughed. "Unfortunately, I lost the better one."

Still, she couldn't help but admire the perfectly forged steel in the morning light.

"I think the buffalo are getting tired," Cerberus said as he swung the reins again. Sure enough, the buffalo were slowing down. They weren't built for high-speed adventures after all.

"We can make our way through the narrows," said Bernadina. "Let's hop off here."

Passing a cluster of buildings, everyone disembarked from the carriage. With a final crack of the reins, Cerberus sent it moving on its own way in the opposite direction of where they were headed—a hopeful mislead for anyone who may have been following in pursuit.

"Be careful to avoid any statues of the king in town. They say he uses them to spy," Bernadina said. "Now follow me. I'm the only one of you that's from around here."

Sal carried both Northsie and Herring in his mechanical arms as the group made their way through the narrow alleys of Cathorn. Northsie rubbed her burned ankle and tried to squeeze out from Sal's hold.

"Could you put me down," Northsie asked. "I want to help, too."

"You're injured," Sal replied. "And if your ankle gets worse, you'll be no help to anyone. We need to take care of it."

"I should've helped more before," she said. "I was protecting the wrong community. It's my fault that Johnsto's gone."

"Northsie," Cerberus replied, "Johnsto was —"

"Shhh," hissed Bernadina. "If any of you want to actually help, stop talking and watch our backs."

Message received; the group continued. Northsie adjusted herself so that she could watch over Sal's rear shoulder. Various folks were emerging from their homes, cautious yet curious to see what all the commotion was about.

"The castle, it's gone!"

"I don't believe it."

"We should get inside. Hide somewhere safe until we know what's going on."

Cerberus looked back across Cathorn and up towards the ruins strewn across the mountain side. It was hard to believe that earlier that day a proud castle had stood in that very spot.

"I can't believe the dragon is finally gone," he whispered to Leonidas as they walked.

"We can't be too sure, little one," Leonidas replied.

"Well, after you were taken, I could feel a tingle in my spine every time the dragon was near," Cerberus said, "But today, for the first time in ten years, I don't feel anything at all."

"Still, let's not celebrate quite yet," Leonidas said.

Soon, the group arrived at Bernadina's house. They slipped inside unnoticed, locking the door behind them.

"It sure is dusty in here," Leonidas said, shielding a sneeze as he looked at the layers of dust that decorated the room.

"We can't stay here very long," Bernadina said, ignoring him. "We need to figure out our plan quickly."

"Our plan? What happened to our plan back at the castle?" Cerberus asked. "You destroyed the portal!"

"Of course I destroyed the portal," Bernadina retorted. "Everything changed the moment the king brought the castle to life and connected himself directly to the portal. How were we supposed to kill the dragon then? You know as well as I do that destroying the portal was the only opportunity we had."

She bustled around her home, checking to see if anything had been disturbed during her time away. Once satisfied, she hurried over to her cauldron to heat up some roast on the open fire. She set a large jug of water out along with some mugs, and everyone helped themselves to a much-needed drink.

"Sometimes you have to stick to the plan," she continued. "But other times you need to do what's right."

"I mean, you're right," Cerberus said, " I just wish it had all played out the way I thought it would in my head."

"Cerberus," Leonidas called softly, and he turned to see Northsie sitting down at the dining table, her head in her arms, disturbing a thick layer of dust from a seat that hadn't been sat in in years. Leonidas pulled out the adjacent seat, and joined her, putting his paw on her shoulder for support.

"Northsie, what happened to Johnsto isn't your fault," Cerberus said as he joined them. "He saved all of us."

"I know that's not my fault," Northsie replied through muffled sniffs. "But I let him down. I let you down."

"You didn't let me down," Cerberus said.

"Yes, I did," Northsie replied. "You were at my Choring-of-Age ceremony. When I added my name to the community chore wheel, I pledged that I would support and care for my community, through the completion of my daily chores."

"These weren't chores, Northsie," Cerberus spoke quietly.

"Yes. They were." Northsie looked up with resolve. "The most important daily chore is practicing care and support for each other. Especially when your community is in trouble."

She took a deep breath to center herself.

"I thought I needed to join King Luridae's community. I thought that was the only way. But, if I had kept my pledge, Johnsto might..."

"You're here now, Northsie," Cerberus said, comforting her. "And Johnsto knew what he was doing. He did it to protect you. You're the future of Bismarthi. It's not too late to keep your pledge."

"We've all made mistakes," Bernadina said quietly.

She had been so quiet Cerberus had almost forgotten she was still in the room.

"Northsie, all of us here have made mistakes. We've all lost the communities we came from. Leonidas and Cerberus from their world, Sal from his, you from Bismarthi, my family..."

Her words trailed off as she became lost in thought. Quickly she pulled herself back out of it.

"But unlike the rest of us, you still have Bismarthi, Northsie. It may be far, but it's still there. And we can still get you home, even if we can't do anything else. We can still return you to your community."

"Bernadina is right," Cerberus said. "We've lost the portal. My dad and I have no way of getting home now. But we still need to get out of Cathorn before the king finds us. You're the only one of us who has a community that we have any chance of returning to. Can we return with you and possibly join your community too?"

"I would be honored," Northsie said, standing up and wiping the few tears that had remained on her cheeks. "Johnsto would be honored, too. Clora and the others will be overjoyed to see you again."

"All in favor of going to Bismarthi?" Cerberus asked the room.

"Yes." Everyone agreed.

"All right, we need to move now," Bernadina said as she watched the street carefully through a small hole next to a boarded-up window. "We don't have long. Let's grab some supplies, whatever you can carry. We'll find a new carriage and depart at once. It's going to be a long ride."

Bernadina crossed the room to open a cabinet. She pulled out a large rolled up sheet of parchment. Unraveling it, she held it up for everyone to see. It was a hand painted map of Cathorn.

"My father drafted this map himself," she said. "He spent years exploring every pathway through the city, carefully charting his findings. He didn't trust the official maps; he said they were incomplete. Maybe we can use this to find a way to escape the city unseen."

Cerberus looked up at the massive portrait of Bernadina's family that hung above the mantle of the stone fireplace. Five raccoons, standing in a formal family pose. Bernadina's parents, her older siblings, and tiny Bernadina, clutching her mother's paw lovingly.

Bernadina pulled out a compass and a few other mapping tools. Sal joined her, disturbing the dust on the table as he made space for them to work. "I can help complete this," he said, using his extending mechanical arms to pin the map open. "I charted out the entire region for King Luridae back when Cathorn began. I know the lost routes that were hidden. I'm the one who was asked to hide them."

Leonidas sneezed again.

"Sorry," he said, "Bernadina, I don't mean to be rude. It's just a little hard for me to breath in here with all of this dust everywhere."

"Yeah, why is it so dusty in here?" Northsie asked.

"It's a long story," said Bernadina, "One I don't have the time or interest to explain right now."

Cerberus walked over to the portrait for another, closer, look. From what he could gather, Bernadina's family appeared to be as kind and caring as she was. He ran his paw across the edge of the portrait frame, picking up a thick layer of dust. Yet as dusty as the room was, the fireplace below was unusually clean.

"Bernadina," he said cautiously, "I know we thought Maximo had thrown your family into the incinerator, but now that we know that isn't true, I just don't see how or why your family would have left you behind. There must be more to this."

"There is still plenty of roast left, and it's going to be a while before we eat something hot again," Bernadina said, as she refilled everyone's bowls, ignoring Cerberus's question. "As soon as we're done eating, we have to leave. Sal, have you figured out a good route?"

"All set," Sal reported back.

"Brogdalio keeps a few carts at the inn near the edge of town," Bernadina said, topping off Northsie's bowl of stew. "We'll take one of those. He owes me a couple of paychecks anyway."

Leonidas picked up his bowl of stew. He fed a spoonful to Herring, who honked happily.

"Cerberus, aren't you hungry? You haven't touched your food."

Cerberus looked at Bernadina as she held a full bowl out for him. It certainly was strange that she cooked over a fire across the room, when the fireplace he was standing next to clearly had enough space to hold the cauldron.

"Bernadina," Cerberus asked, "why do you do your cooking over there, and not in this fireplace?"

"Well, because this is my kitchen, and that's the formal fireplace," she replied, almost sarcastically. "You don't cook in the formal fireplace. My family was very big on keeping separate spaces in the home."

Cerberus looked at the fireplace closely. "So, you don't use this fireplace at all?"

"No. I haven't touched it in years. Do you want some roast or not? We've got to go."

"If you haven't used it at all," Cerberus asked, "why isn't it dusty inside?"

Bernadina put down the roast. She picked up her other supplies as she made her way to the door.

"When I was little, my parents told me not to go near it, so I still don't. Now, come on."

"But then… why is it so clean?"

Cerberus kneeled. He reached inside the fireplace and gave the back a rub with his paw. He felt a faint sensation, almost like static electricity. He pulled his paw back out and compared it to the one that had rubbed the dusty picture frame moments earlier.

It really was strange. Though everything surrounding the fireplace carried a thick layer of dust, the inside of the fireplace was perfectly clean—almost as if it had just been installed that day. The surrounding dust went right to the edge of the hearth, but then cut off sharply. Inside the fireplace, the stone was clean enough to eat off.

"Bernadina, what happened to your family?" Sal asked, joining Cerberus in investigation.

"I told you we need to leave now, but since you insist on wasting valuable time, fine, I guess now is as good a time as any for a story," Bernadina replied annoyed. "They too were inspired by Alaine Dubeck and helped citizens escape the reign of King Luridae by smuggling them out of Cathorn. But the king caught on, and he sent Maximo and his guards to capture them, along with the other revolutionaries."

Bernadina took a breath.

"I was working a long shift for Brogdalio the day it happened. I came home, and they were gone. Not a trace. Just taken like so many others. I never heard from them again."

"Do you know where your parents were sending the folks they rescued?" Leonidas asked.

"No," Bernadina said. "All I know is that they said the destination couldn't be close, otherwise the king would find them again. It was a secret that only my parents knew. They never told me. They said if anyone else knew, it wouldn't be safe."

As Bernadina spoke, Herring waddled his way into the fireplace and began to honk softly, pressing against the farthest bricks.

"What does he want?" Bernadina asked. "Why is he going in

there?"

"He's acting like there's something on the other side." Sal said.

"I'll tell you what's on the other side," Bernadina snapped. "The street. The wind. The cold. The path to Bismarthi. Where *we* should be heading. We need to leave *now*."

Northsie stood, eager to help Bernadina finish packing. Sal pulled his mechanical arms out of the fireplace.

"There's a strong energy reading coming from here, but it's unfamiliar—even to me," he said.

Herring honked again from inside the fireplace. The little penguin had his wings pressed up against the back wall as hard as he could.

"Okay, let's get you out of there," Sal said, reaching back into the fireplace to pick up Herring.

Without warning, a flash of energy whipped out of Sal's mechanical hands and into the fireplace, temporarily blinding everyone with bright golden light. Slowly, the room came back into focus.

Herring was gone.

"Herring!"

Everyone gathered quickly, trying to find the little penguin who had vanished without a trace.

"Where did he go?" Leonidas asked. "Sal, what was that energy? Did you generate that?"

"No, I don't know what happened," Sal said. "It felt like a flow of energy came through the fireplace and grabbed hold of my body's power cells. I've never felt or seen anything like it."

"I know that light…"

Cerberus turned to see Bernadina setting her bags back down against the wall in disbelief. For being ready to urgently leave, her tone had changed, and Cerberus saw a look in her eyes that he had never seen before.

"I remember when I was young, my family had a friend,"

Bernadina said. "His name was Old Martinian, and he and my father used to joke over dinner about their hopes, dreams, and ways they could change the world."

Bernadina walked over to the fireplace and rested her paw on the mantle.

"One night, Old Martinian was over for dinner, and my parents sent me to bed early." Bernadina continued. "As I was falling asleep, I remember seeing a flash of golden light that spilled under my doorway. It was gone a moment later, but it was so bright, so unusual, I've never forgotten it."

Bernadina took a deep breath.

"Two days later, my father told me that Old Martinian had been killed by the king's soldiers in the streets, and a few days after that we attended his funeral."

Bernadina averted her eyes. Leonidas took her paw in his own for support as he looked into her eyes.

"Forgive me if I sound insensitive," Leonidas began, "But is it possible, that Old Martinian's funeral was faked?"

"All I know is that night was the first and only time I have ever seen that golden light. I know it's the same one."

Cerberus knew there wasn't a lot of time, and while being polite always has its place, he figured that this was one of those moments when getting to the point quickly and without pleasantries would be appropriate. It seemed obvious enough, and after his father's question about Old Martinian's funeral, there was no harm in asking another possibly insensitive question.

"Is it possible that this fireplace is another type of portal?"

Everyone turned to Cerberus, but he kept his eyes locked on Bernadina's. Her expression said it all, and even if she didn't know all the pieces in this puzzle, they were adding up quickly to Cerberus.

"Bernadina, what were you working on when you first brought me here?" Cerberus asked.

"You mean my personal business?" Bernadina replied.

"Bernadina, come on."

"Okay."

Bernadina went to her drawer, and unlocking it, pulled out the device she had been tinkering with. It was a rudimentary device made of a fusion of brass and gold; various inputs each connected to a vial containing a viscous, golden liquid, not unlike thick honey.

"I found this thing in the fireplace the day my family vanished. I never knew what it was. As much as I've tried, I have never been able to activate it on my own. It's the only clue I have as to what may have happened to them."

Sal spoke. "When I reached inside the fireplace, I could feel an energy surge, something different, yet similar to what we used in our portal. Maybe this device is the key."

"So, you're telling me there might be a portal in my fireplace?" Bernadina said, raising an eyebrow. "I think I would know if there was a portal in my fireplace."

She passed the device to Sal.

"But let's say you're right and there is. Can you turn it on?"

"I'm not sure," Sal replied. "I haven't seen this type of technology before. It's not anything like the portal we built. It doesn't even seem like it uses MonFus as a power source. I need more time to study it."

"Well then we can't leave yet," Cerberus said, standing. "If there's any chance that Bernadina's family could have used this, this may be the only way to find them again. We need to get this thing up and running now."

"Cerberus, if the king finds us here, we're all dead," Bernadina said. "My family is already gone. I can't put all of you in harm's way, too."

"No," Cerberus replied. "Nobody gets left behind."

Cerberus pulled the UltraNine out of his pocket. He looked over at Leonidas, remembering how he had used the tool to fuse the MonFus with the giraffe proof and power their portal all those years ago.

"Dad, do you think we could use this to connect and activate the power sources on this portal? Could we calibrate it to reconnect to its last assigned destination?"

Leonidas smiled at his son. "If anything can get the job done, The Creator's Pen can."

"The device activated when I put my hands in the fireplace," Sal said. "Pass me the laser, let me see what I can do."

A loud boom outside stirred the layers of dust as Cerberus passed the UltraNine to Sal, who quickly got to work connecting the device to the fireplace.

"Hurry, Sal!" Cerberus called. "We have to get Bernadina out of here."

"Wait, what do you mean?" Bernadina asked. "I thought we were going to bring them back here!"

A second boom echoed over the first, stirring up even more dust. It sounded much closer. Sal worked diligently, and the fireplace portal power device began to glow with soft, golden energy pulses.

"No, we all need to get out of Cathorn," Cerberus said. "If your family is on the other side of that portal, that's where you need to go."

"No!" Bernadina said. "If I leave, I'll be abandoning all of you. Can't you come with me? If we all leave together—"

"We'd be abandoning the other folks of Cathorn," Cerberus said. "They need us now."

"Not even Bismarthi will be safe from the king's fury," Northsie said.

"We're the only ones who know the truth about the king and this place," Cerberus said. "Once we're safe, we can regroup. Then we can form a plan to—"

A third boom sounded; nearly shaking the heavy wood door off its hinges. From the other side, an unmistakable voice spoke loudly and confidently.

"Traitors of Cathorn!" Maximo boomed. "By order of King Luridae Igneous, you are to be imprisoned, tortured, and executed, for your dissent to the kingdom, and for your actions against our beloved king. You will be forgotten, and in such the Kingdom of

Cathorn will continue to prosper."

"Quick, turn that off." Bernadina motioned to Sal, who deactivated the UltraNine and handed it back to Cerberus. Instantly the golden glow vanished as the device calmed.

"Bernadina, what are you doing?" Cerberus was confused. "We're trying to get you out of here."

"Let's get through this together," Bernadina said. "And then we'll turn this portal on. Together."

Another boom sounded and the door shook violently again. The wall cracked, losing the frame and hinges in turn. It wouldn't hold for much longer. Cerberus raised his UltraNine, adjusting the dial slowly.

"Everyone, stand behind me."

30

Boom! The door frame finally gave way, and the hinges snapped off as the heavy wooden slab fell to the ground. Maximo entered slowly, armor trailing smoke with each step.

"I knew you'd crawl back here." He smirked at Bernadina as his paw grasped the handle of her sword on his hip. The purple gem flashed from the hilt, mocking them.

"I know what happened to my parents," Bernadina spouted back. "You're weaker than you think."

"I thought you were simply traitors," Maximo said. "But you're something else entirely. Return to the castle ruins. The king will raise the castle once again, and we will rebuild the portal. It's rare, but the king can be forgiving. Coming with me is your best chance."

Cerberus couldn't help but laugh. Maximo glared back in response. He drew the golden sword from his hilt enough to make a point. It still glowed from the battle earlier.

"How dare you," Maximo said. "Now, all of you, come with me at once."

"No," Cerberus replied, UltraNine raised.

Behind Maximo, Bernadina looked over at the supplies she'd just set down moments before. The sword she had taken in the escape, Maximo's own, lay next to it.

"No," Cerberus stated again. "You think that after everything we've gone through to get this far, we're going to go back and build a new portal for King Luridae? You think we're going to go back to being your prisoners? No way."

"Speaking of the king, where is he?" Sal asked from the corner.

"King Luridae does not need you alive. That was merely a gesture of kindness," Maximo said. He approached Cerberus, the smoke on his armor darkening with each step.

"King Luridae has always existed and will always continue to. If you die here today, the king will simply wait until the time comes that you are born and find you before you even become aware of his existence. You can help him now, or you can help him later. There are no other options."

Maximo pulled the golden sword and swung, but in a flash, Bernadina darted in, shoving Cerberus aside while grabbing the steel one and parrying the blow. Cerberus stumbled back, short of breath from the near miss.

Using Maximo's own sword, Bernadina pushed the golden blade back, forcing him towards the cauldron. But, an expert swordsman, he stepped back, confidently navigating around her blade. They exchanged blows once again, Bernadina matching him as best she could.

"You got this!" Cerberus rooted.

Bernadina swung again. Maximo twisted his sword hilt in defense, unintentionally splitting the golden blade into three. Bernadina's sword was knocked from her paw. It flew across the room, landing directly in the fire under the cauldron.

Maximo twisted the hilt back with a smirk, merging the blade back into one. Raising it above his head he lunged at Bernadina. Sal leapt forward, using his mechanical legs to propel himself. Upon collision, Sal pushed Maximo back, and Northsie extended her leg, tripping him. As he fell, golden sword slipped out of his paw and flipped up into the air. Heavy blade pointed towards the earth, it picked up speed as it fell into Maximo's chest, hissing as it pierced through his armor. Taking advantage of the opportunity, Bernadina grabbed golden handle and twisted it. The blade promptly split into three, and the armor flashed as the steam was pulled from it, sucked into the gem.

Maximo opened his mouth in a silent scream as he instantly dissolved, vanishing into nothing. Only a few wisps of him lingered in the air before they, too, were drawn into the gem. His armor rolled across the floor, empty and powerless.

"I'll take that back, thank you," Bernadina said. She pulled her sword from the chitin armor and returned it to her hip where it belonged. The golden gem still glowed pulsed with energy.

"If I'd known that sword was down there the whole time, maybe I would've been able to escape sooner," Leonidas commented.

"Bernadina, are you okay?" Cerberus asked.

But Bernadina was already back over at the fireplace, fiddling with the golden portal device.

"We've got to get out of here," she urged. "*Now*."

Sal and Cerberus gathered to help Bernadina, as booms of falling stone and shaking earth continued outside. Northsie and Leonidas propped up the wooden door, blocking the opening it had once been secured to.

"The technology in here is something I've never seen. I don't know how your parents figured out how to do what they did," Sal said. "But they sure knew what they were doing."

"Yeah," Bernadina said. "I guess they did."

"Alright Cerberus, turn on the UltraNine and aim it right here," Sal said, gesturing. "It's time to power this thing up."

"On it," Cerberus confirmed as he pointed the laser into the fireplace at the golden device carefully and activated it.

Slowly the golden device began to radiate a bright glow as it charged. The device flashed with light, and with a crack, bolts of golden lightning emanated out, forming the outline of a doorway, perfectly sized to fit the fireplace. The golden portal flashed open.

"Alright, I think you can turn the UltraNine off now," Sal said.

Cerberus deactivated the laser as everyone stared into the newly formed portal in awe. The other side came slowly into view; an older raccoon taking a step out of the other side. He turned around with a surprised glance.

"Bernadina? Is that you?" he asked. "But you're older! Who are all these folks?"

Bernadina's eyes welled with tears as she saw her father for the first time in years. "Dad," she said. "It's been so long."

"I thought you were at work," he said. "The guards are on their way. You need to come through now, or we're all lost."

"Dad," Bernadina said, "it's been years. We—"

"Oh no," the older racoon's eyes grew wide in fear. "What's that?"

Maximo's helmet trembled where it had fallen. Slowly, its surface began to warp, glowing brighter and brighter until it blazed white-hot. The molten heat spread outward, consuming the fallen armor piece by piece.

Then, the armor began to rise. Liquid fire surged up from the boots, fusing the scattered pieces together. Beneath it, the earth rumbled. A fissure split open, magma pooling and rising, climbing into the hollow shell. It filled the gaps, giving shape and mass to the form until, at last, the helmet locked into place.

"You have to get out of here!" Bernadina yelled at her father through the golden portal door. "Sal, how do we shut thing off?"

"Too late," a familiar deep voice growled.

From within, molten metal dripped downward, sculpting the face of King Luridae—his visage searing itself into the form where Maximo's had once been. His eyes flared a blazing orange-white, snapping open with sudden awareness. Molten magma dripped from his mouth as it twisted into a menacing smile.

"Nobody told me you had another portal," King Luridae rumbled as he stalked forward in the dark basalt armor, the puddle of magma below him flowing along with each step. "I knew it was worth waiting to reveal myself."

"You can leave the castle?" Cerberus asked breathlessly.

"I can do a lot of things I haven't told you about," King Luridae smiled.

Bernadina drew her golden sword and struck, aiming to catch the king off guard. But with a swift counter, King Luridae snatched the blade between his molten claws. She twisted the hilt, and the sword split apart, tearing through his fiery grip, and flinging specks of magma into the air.

Yet, as quickly as his claw was destroyed, it reformed. With confidence, he seized two of the three sundered blades, pressing forward with unstoppable force. At last, he wrenched the weapon from her grasp and flung it aside, the mangled remnants clattering against the far wall of the room.

"Stop!" Cerberus yelled.

King Luridae's whipped his head around in furious response. His beady glowing eyes started directly into Cerberus own.

"Can't you see you've lost everything," Cerberus said. "You have nothing now. No castle. No dragon. No army."

"I am my own army," King Luridae growled.

By command, the molten pool beneath King Luridae's feet spread, stretching across the room. From its glowing depths, several faceless copies of the king began to rise, their bodies forming from the seething lava. Still, they remained tethered to the ever-shifting magma pool, never straying from its reach.

As they advanced, the copies herded the group toward the pulsing yellow portal, their heat intensifying with every step. Flames caught on the wooden beams overhead, spreading fast, turning Bernadina's home into a deadly inferno.

"Cerberus!" Sal shouted. "The UltraNine!"

Without hesitation, Cerberus drew the handheld laser, twisting the dial to widen the beam. Upon release, the brilliant energy sliced through one of the molten copies, severing it from the main pool. Instantly, the fiery form darkened, hardening into lifeless basalt.

"What?!" King Luridae recoiled.

The king bellowed as his living magma surged toward the frozen husk, desperate to reclaim it. But it was useless. The lava splashed against the hardened stone, unable to reabsorb what had been lost. For the first time, the king's molten fury flickered with something new—uncertainty.

"It worked! I don't know how, but it worked!" Sal cheered.

The molten puddle shifted as the remaining copies charged the group. Cerberus swung the UltraNine around as quickly as he could, releasing carefully calibrated energy as quickly as possible to protect the group from the onslaught of attacks. As severed pieces fell, they cooled and hardened instantly, unable to be reclaimed by the king's efforts.

"Keep going!" yelled Bernadina.

Cerberus dropped to the ground and swung the beam directly at the king's ankles. All the remaining copies separated and froze into lifeless basalt statues instantly as King Luridae lost his footing and fell on his back, the room continuing to burn around him.

Struggling, the molten king pushed himself upright, reshaping into a snakelike molten form in place of his previous one. But Cerberus was relentless. He kept swinging, and piece after piece of King Luridae fell away, reducing him more and more with each slicing beam of light. The king attempted to take new form after new form, shifting to avoid the laser, growing smaller and smaller by the second.

With a powerful swing of the UltraNine, Cerberus severed the king's head. It fell with a molten splat, dripping out of Maximo's helmet, as the remaining body that had once lived below it froze permanently place.

It seemed the king finally had found something to fear, as the molten remainder slid around the floor, looking for new material to fuse with.

"Cerberus!" Sal shouted over the roaring flames. "If he touches anything molten, he'll recover instantly!"

Cerberus kept slicing, the laser carving through the molten mass, breaking it down again and again. The glowing form shrank with each cut until, at last, a single cobalt-blue scorpion, veins pulsing with magma, emerged from the final splash of liquid rock.

Small but fast, King Luridae's core form darted forward, its red-hot stinger dripping with molten fire.

Instinct took over—Cerberus swiped with his paw, sending the scorpion flying into the stone wall. It hit hard but was stunned for only a moment before it scrambled upright, its tail tapping frantically against the ground.

"It's searching for more matter to fuse with!" Sal warned. "If it finds a way to connect to any new material—"

Before he could finish, the scorpion launched itself off the edge of a dish, soaring through the air—straight for the golden portal.

"No!" Cerberus leapt towards it, missing the catch as the scorpion flew.

Fueled by impulse, Bernadina grabbed the water jug from the nearby table, hurling the contents across the room, dousing the flying scorpion with cold water, freezing it into a stone state instantly.

The petrified scorpion fell to the ground, mere inches from the golden portal door. Wisps of steam emanated as Sal picked up the former king in his mechanical claws, and everyone quickly gathered for a closer look. Even though the scorpion appeared still and lifeless, a faint pulse continued to radiate out from deep within.

"I can't believe we finally stopped him," Sal said. "I truly thought it might be impossible."

"I used to think a lot of things were impossible," Cerberus replied. "But I don't know if I think anything is impossible anymore."

"The king's reign of terror is finally over," said Leonidas. "Well done little one."

"I'll be sure to keep this safe," Sal said with a grin. His mechanical body whirred, and a small compartment on his chest sprang open. What remained of the king was quickly and safely stored away.

Cerberus touched his face to wipe off the sweat from the heat of the moment, but the sweat felt cold, and almost refreshing. He felt another drop, and wiping his brow, looked up. This wasn't sweat.

Snow was falling through the collapsed roof, putting out the fire and washing the dust off the surviving furniture inside the house as it turned to condensation on landing.

Cerberus and Northsie rushed to the door of the house, pulling back the heavy slab that blocked it. Together, they looked up at the mountaintop where the castle had once stood. One by one, the citizens of Cathorn cautiously emerged from their homes. Though the locals weren't sure exactly what had happened, a wave of relief swept through the city. As snowflakes landed on cheeks, they quickly melted into water, and no one could tell if anyone else was crying tears of happiness or if the moisture was simply clinging to their faces with unusual intensity.

On the other side of the golden portal, Herring was getting some belly scratches from Bernadina's dad and honking happily. The little racoon made her way across her ruined home, returning to her side of the glowing doorway.

"I can't believe you defeated King Luridae," Bernadina's dad said.

"Without your daughter's help, none of this would be possible," Cerberus said, joining her side.

"Bernadina, I always knew you had greatness in you," her dad responded. "This is a truly historic moment. I'm so glad I got to witness it."

"When are you?" Bernadina asked. "Where does this portal go?"

"Before the First Moments," said Bernadina's dad. "The only way we could escape King Luridae was if we came back to before he ever became king. It was the only way real way to escape. Now, come on through and join us."

"Why don't you come back here?" Bernadina asked. "The king is gone. It's safe."

"Secretly, we've been establishing a village here, a society with everything we need," Bernadina's dad said. "You'll understand when you come through here and see this place. The water is clean. The crops are safe. There are no toxins or pollution. Whenever we knew King Luridae was pursuing someone in Cathorn, we tried to smuggle them through here. Our friends and family are here. Why would we ever come back?"

"But how could you leave without me?" Bernadina asked, holding the tears that were welling up in her eyes.

"We didn't want to," Bernadina's dad said, not holding his own tears back. "But it was an emergency. You mom and siblings went through, and I tried to wait, but if I had waited any longer, the king would've found not only us but our new village as well, and then none of us would've survived. We knew Brogdalio would look out for you. We knew you would be safe without us."

"But I don't want to be," Bernadina said as tears began to fall.

"I know that for you it's been a long time since you've seen us," Bernadina's father said as he extended his paw through the golden door of the portal. "But, for me, I just saw you this morning. Let's not lose any more time."

Bernadina turned to Cerberus. "Thank you," she said, "for not leaving me behind. Without you—without all of you, I may never have found my family again."

"Bernadina, you took me in when I was freezing at your doorstep. You listened to me. You helped me. I would never have found my father again if not for you. You've done so much for me, for my family, for all of us."

Cerberus sniffed as tears welled up in his eyes. Bernadina gave him a big hug.

"I wish we didn't have to go our separate ways now," Cerberus said. "Hopefully we'll see each other again."

"We will," Bernadina said confidently. Turning back towards the golden portal, she stopped in front of Sal.

"Sal, you should come with me," she said. "Isn't this your original time? Where you belong?"

"You'll be safer there," Sal said. "But I think my knowledge is better served here."

Bernadina nodded, and with that she took her dads paw and followed him into the portal. Herring honked with joy.

"Ya know, I think you might be our oldest cubbin now," Bernadina's dad said with a chuckle.

"She's going to be an incredible role model," Leonidas said. "We'll all miss you dearly."

Sal adjusted the golden vial, closing the portal door. As it fizzled out, Bernadina turned back for a final wave.

Then, she was gone.

31

Cerberus turned to Sal. "So, can we figure out how adjust this portal's destination so me and my dad can finally go home?" he asked.

"Well, there's still one problem," Leonidas said quietly.

"What do you mean?" Cerberus asked. "What's the problem?"

"We don't have any of the dragon's molt. Without the MonFus, we can't pick the specific moment in time that we want to return to," Leonidas replied. "We can only return to the exact moment when we each last went through it."

"So, what's the problem with that?" Cerberus asked impatiently.

"Well, I left ten years before you did," Leonidas said. "Which means, even if we can adjust this portal's destination to take us home, if we both walk through at the same time, we'll each find ourselves returned to the different moments in time when we individually left."

"And if that happens, everything we've accomplished will be undone," Sal said.

"That means the dragon will still be here," Cerberus said. "That means King Luridae will still be here."

"Exactly," Sal confirmed. "We're trying to change the timeline, not just travel through it. And for that, we need MonFus."

Cerberus rubbed his face with his paws in frustration.

"It's impossible," he said. "It would take forever to find the scale deposit, and it's not like we can go digging around in the ruins of the collapsed castle to try to find the dragons remains."

Cerberus kicked one of the pieces of Maximo's fallen armor. It slid across the room, settling next to the crumpled remains of Bernadina's golden sword in the corner.

"Wait—" Cerberus said as he crossed the room to examine it more closely. Though the sword was beyond repair, the purple gem was still glowing strongly.

"Remember how this gem sucked the essence out of Maximo and the other guards armor?" he asked.

"How could I forget?" said Leonidas.

"It was horrifying," said Northsie.

Cerberus set the gem down on the table. Smoky blue electric energy coursed through the purple gem. Sal, Northsie, and Leonidas gathered around to examine it more closely.

"Is it possible this gem is retaining the energy it pulled from the MonFus in the guards' armor?" Cerberus asked.

"The armor?" Sal asked curiously. "There's MonFus in the armor?"

"Yeah," Cerberus said, "Bernadina and I saw the guards rubbing their armor with MonFus, to enhance it or something. I don't know what it did, but it seemed to make their armor stronger."

"They kept it a secret from the king," said Northsie, "and threated to hurt anyone if they told."

Sal smiled.

"Cerberus, pass me that gem and your UltraNine," Sal said. "I think you and your dad are going home today after all."

32

With a few careful adjustments, Sal was able to use the UltraNine to connect the gem to golden device so that the MonFus could be transferred over. Once infused, the portal door shifted, and its glow changed from golden to a more greenish tint.

Sal plucked a hair from both Cerberus and Leonidas respectively, and using the UltraNine, fused them together into a new proof, which glowed a familiar red. Adding it to the device, the portal door color shifted again, blending with the greenish tint to glow a darker purple-brown.

"I know it may not be beautiful, but we're working with what we've got," Sal said with a chuckle as he continued to tinker. Northsie, Cerberus, and Leonidas gathered in front of the portal as the other side began to materialize into view. The other side was very unclear.

"Once you step through this door, you should both find yourself back home together, just moments after Cerberus originally left," Sal said.

"That'll work," Cerberus said, barely able to contain his excitement.

"However, you won't be *where* you were when you left," said Sal. "You'll emerge in the same place we are now, just in your own time. This isn't a two-way portal, once you go through there is no coming back."

"After we see you off, I'll continue with Northsie to Bismarthi," Sal said.

"Keep each other safe," said Leonidas. He smiled kindly at Northsie.

"We will," Northsie said. "I won't ever abandon my community again."

"I know you were only trying to survive," Cerberus said. "But it's easier when you stick together."

He gave Northsie a gentle hug. He was going to miss her a lot. He wished he could return to Bismarthi with her, to see Clora, Massimo, Parlie, Jacoby, Galletta, and the others again. He wanted to help build the new water tower, and he looked forward to seeing what they would be able to accomplish and build without having to spend so much time keeping the fire burning every night anymore.

"Everything is going to change now that you no longer need to live in fear of the dragon and King Luridae," Leonidas said, "Once we're back home, we look forward to seeing all that you've accomplished written in history."

"Thank you for including me in your community, Northsie," Cerberus said. "When I had nobody, the folk of Bismarthi saved me. We wouldn't be here now if not for them. Or you. I'm proud I got to bear witness to your Choring-of-Age."

"I hope you return to Bismarthi one day," Northsie said, "even if it's in your own time. I'll tell your story. I'll make sure you are always remembered and welcome."

Leonidas threw a warm arm over Sal's mechanical shoulder.

"Should I finally tell you that we meet in the future again?" he asked with a cheeky smile.

"There's no way I would ever stop keeping an eye on you," Sal laughed.

"It's been great getting to know you for the past twenty-five years," Leonidas said. "But I'm sure not going to miss this place."

"Get out of here," Sal said. "It's time to go. I'll see you when I see you."

"Destroy this portal after we're gone," Leonidas said. "We'll handle the one on our end. We don't need anything else coming through this time."

"Way ahead of you," Sal said. "With the castle and our research gone, I'm the only one with any knowledge of how to build these things, and I don't intend to share it with anyone."

Leonidas and Sal laughed together once more. Sal returned the UltraNine to Cerberus, who thoughtfully and securely placed it in his pocket.

"Alright little one," Leonidas said, "are you ready?"

Cerberus took one last look around the ruined room. The statues of the copies of King Luridae, the fallen armor, the warm pot of stew, the family portrait that—though badly burned—was still recognizable, Sal's mechanical body, Northsie's warm smile. He looked up at the sky through the ceiling and took a deep breath as a final snowflake settled on the tip of his nose. He turned to his father, the reason he had gone through this whole journey, and took his paw in his own tightly.

"I am."

And with that, Leonidas and Cerberus kneeled and together, they entered the purple-brown portal in the fireplace.

✳ ✳ ✳

Cerberus stood up, bumping his head on a shelf. Disoriented, he stood up, helping Leonidas out behind him. As soon as they were both through, the door closed, vanishing instantly.

The room was dark. Cerberus felt around, hoping to find a light switch. "I hope we're in the right place," he muttered.

"You can trust Sal," Leonidas said.

Cerberus's paw felt a switch and he clicked it on. Looking around the shelves of pots, pans, and other cookware, everything felt very familiar.

As Cerberus's eyes adjusted to the light, he and Leonidas pushed back the double chef doors that opened into a long, familiar hallway.

"What are we doing at the Culinary Academy?" he wondered aloud.

At the far end, a student of about Cerberus's age came around the corner.

"Hey, Cerberus! I thought you'd be halfway home by now," the student said with a laugh. "But I know how hard it's going to be for you to leave this place."

The student continued through the double doors into the very room they had just exited.

Leonidas smiled. "Did you just graduate this year?"

"I did… this past spring," Cerberus said as he slowly remembered what year it was. "I had almost completely forgotten."

"Look at that. Mixing and rearranging things just like I used to do in the lab," Leonidas laughed. "But your line of work is a lot less dangerous."

"Hey, one of my classmates lost a finger once," Cerberus protested. "Those knives are sharp."

"Sorry I missed your graduation," Leonidas said quietly.

Cerberus remembered many events that Leonidas had missed. But it was all right; there would be many new memories they could make now, together.

Exciting the Culinary Academy, Cerberus looked up at the nearby hills, covered with homes, shops, and roads in plain view. To Cerberus, those hills had been mountains just moments ago, home to the castle of King Luridae.

Cerberus wondered how many years had passed since the castle had fallen. He wondered if there was anyone alive who knew the history. Certainly, he'd never been taught about it as a young kidden.

"So that's where you got the MonFus to open the first portal," Cerberus said, turning to Leonidas, who was staring off into the hills as well.

"If only I had known what was on the other side," Leonidas said, "I might have never tried to build the portal in the first place."

Cerberus thought about the paradox that *"not opening the portal"* ten years ago would've created. It seemed that the discovery had been inevitable and unavoidable. If the portal had never been opened, would the castle still stand today? Would King Luridae still reign?

"Even though we lost time," Cerberus replied to his father, "I think it's more important that we know the lost history."

Leonidas nodded in agreement.

"I can't help but to think about the king's museum," Leonidas said quietly. "All those objects from both the past and future, lost in the depths of those hills. Who knows what magic, science, or other knowledge we're missing."

"It was probably all destroyed by the magma," Cerberus said. "Any excuse to avoid returning to those hills is good enough for me."

"I suppose you're right."

Leonidas looked at the hills for a moment longer. A quarter-century of memories weren't going to leave as quickly.

"Cerberus?"

Cerberus turned back to the Culinary Academy, just in time to see Dot loading an ice cream incubator into the back of a buffalo taxi.

"Dot! What are you doing here?" Cerberus ran over with a smile.

"Just packing up some of my equipment," she replied with a smile. "Couldn't get everything home in one trip!"

She stopped and stared at him.

"Are you okay? You look terrible. And what are you wearing?"

"This is my dad, Leonidas," Cerberus said, quickly changing the subject.

"So nice to meet you," Dot said, extending her paw. "Cerberus always talks about how inspirational you are."

"Thank you," Leonidas said as tears filled his eyes.

"Do you two need a ride?" Dot offered. "I'm heading back to the same area as you are anyway. I'll be setting off shortly if you'd like to join me."

Cerberus and Leonidas happily accepted.

As the buffalo carriage pulled out into the street, Cerberus realized the roads they were taking felt very similar to the "new one" that Sal had charted out for their planned return to Bismarthi. He wondered if that was a coincidence. It was unlikely.

The trip was a long one. Passing buildings, parks, factories, and more ruins along the way, Cerberus thought about the dense woods that had been here long ago, and how he'd struggled to make his way through them. Whenever Dot offered Cerberus a snack or something to drink, he was thankful not to be rationing it for his own survival anymore. He gently rubbed the leather straps that he had received in Bismarthi that still wrapped his hands. They had protected his paws through more challenges than he ever had expected to face.

He was grateful to still have them.

As the world passed by, Cerberus pictured Sal and Northsie making their way home, following the route that would one day become this very same road. He hoped their journey had been an easy one. They had both been through so much.

Cerberus could only imagine how happy Northsie's parents were when they saw her again, and how sad Clora was when she realized Johnsto hadn't returned with them. He hoped she understood how important his sacrifice had been.

As the journey home neared its end, the city felt larger than Cerberus remembered. The buffalo carriage turned a corner into a once familiar town square, and an unfamiliar statue caught his eye at once. One of a proud buck, leading folk bravely into a clearing. Even though felt new to Cerberus, it was clear that this aged and weathered statue wasn't new to anyone else. Folk sat around the park enjoying sandwiches and salads, barely paying any attention to it. Maybe Cerberus just hadn't noticed it before either.

Cerberus wondered if the statue might be of Alain Dubeck, or even of Johnsto. But it wasn't going anywhere, and he could come back to investigate it another day. Maybe even during a picnic with friends of his own.

The buffalo carriage slowed to a stop as it arrived in front of Lucinda's home. Cerberus and Leonidas thanked Dot for the ride, got out, and stood in front of the door. It felt like a million years had passed since the last time they had stood there together.

On the other side of the door, he knew Lucinda was waiting with Henry B. Orenthall and Stephenson. She hadn't seen Leonidas in ten years, but he hadn't seen her in twenty-five. How would things change now that he was back?

And what about Ricky, who was waiting in his ARL across town, excited for Cerberus to return to help him develop all sorts of new animal-based projects? Cerberus decided then and there that the focus could only be on creating new things for the future, not trying to bring back lost moments of the past.

Cerberus took a deep breath. He didn't know if he was ready to face all this. He had been focused on one goal for so long, he had forgotten it was possible to have others.

But here he was, with his father standing next to him. All his long-standing goals had been achieved and his wildest dreams had been realized. The only way to truly embark down the path in front of him was to start creating some new ones.

Cerberus turned to Leonidas, who was clearly processing his own similar feelings. He caught Cerberus's nervous glance and wrapped his arm around him lovingly.

"Are you ready?" Leonidas asked.

Cerberus nodded and smiled at his father. Seeing that smile once again meant that anything was possible.

The young tiger had spent so many moments in his life standing in front of portals—he knew the only way forward was to take a step and jump in. Except this wasn't another portal. This was life.

Cerberus was ready to face it. He exhaled. He straightened his back with resolve.

He and Leonidas walked towards the door, together.

ABOUT THE AUTHOR

Ezra Edmond is an award-winning filmmaker, author, and animation producer with a passion for big ideas and exciting stories. *The Tiger Saga* is an interconnected story that Ezra has been imagining since around 2009. He is thrilled to finally share the adventures of Cerberus and his quest to reunite with his long-lost father, Leonidas, and looks forward to telling more stories set within this world. Ezra lives in Los Angeles, CA, and enjoys traveling, trying new foods, and spending time with his family, friends, and dog, Sherman.

Find more of Ezra's work at:
www.EzraEdmond.com